HIS GIRL FRIDAY

HIS GIRL FRIDAY

Based on a play by
Ben Hecht
Charles MacArthur

Screenplay by
Charles Lederer

Directed by
Howard Hawks

MAPLE SPRING PUBLISHING

Published 2025 by Maple Spring Publishing

HIS GIRL FRIDAY. Copyright © 2025 Maple Spring Publishing. All rights reserved.

No part of this book may be used, reproduced or transmitted in any manner whatsoever, by any means (electronic, photocopying, recording, or otherwise), without the prior written permission of the author, except in the case of brief quotations embodied in critical articles and reviews. No liability is assumed with respect to the use of the information contained within. Although every precaution has been taken, the author and publisher assume no liability for errors or omissions. Neither is any liability assumed for damages resulting from the use of the information contained herein.

Front cover design by David Rheinhardt of Pyrographx
Interior design by Jason Snyder

Library of Congress Cataloging-in-Publication Data is available upon request

ISBN: 979-8-3505-0119-3

10 9 8 7 6 5 4 3 2 1

HIS GIRL FRIDAY

CAST

Cary Grant *as* Walter Burns
Rosalind Russell *as* Hildy Johnson
Ralph Bellamy *as* Bruce Baldwin
Gene Lockhart *as* Sheriff Hartwell
Porter Hall *as* Murphy
Ernest Truex *as* Bensinger
Cliff Edwards *as* Endicott
Clarence Kolb *as* the Mayor
Roscoe Karns *as* McCue
Frank Jenks *as* Wilson
Regis Toomey *as* Sanders
Abner Biberman *as* Louie
Frank Orth *as* Duffy
John Qualen *as* Earl Williams
Helen Mack *as* Mollie Malloy
Alma Kruger *as* Mrs. Baldwin
Billy Gilbert *as* Joe Pettibone
Pat West *as* Warden Cooley
Edwin Maxwell *as* Dr. Eggelhoffer
Marion Martin *as* Evangeline

We see onscreen the following text:

It all happened in the "Dark Ages" of the newspaper game—when to a reporter "getting that story" justified anything short of murder.

Incidentally you will see in this picture no resemblance to the men and women of the press today.

Ready?

Well, once upon a time . . .

We see and hear the immensely busy city room of the *Morning Post.*

Behind are the elevators. A waist-high iron grill with a gate in it separates the switchboard from the anteroom. A similar grill separates the switchboard from the city room, which stretches on beyond switchboard. Some employees are running around; others are talking on the phone. Copy boys are rushing back and forth from desk to desk. The telephone operators are hard at work.

[Background chattering]

EDITOR 1

Copy boy!

EDITOR 2

Where's the rest of this story?

Maisie and Ruth, two operators, are at the switchboard.

MAISIE

Morning Post. City desk.

RUTH

Morning Post. City desk.

Skinny, probably a reporter, goes out the gate and past the switchboard.

SKINNY

If anyone asks for me, I'm gone out.

Seeing elevator doors about to close, Skinny holds it up and rushes in.

SKINNY

Elevator!

Out of the other elevator come Hildy Johnson, a beautiful and smartly dressed young woman, and Bruce Baldwin, her beau, a handsome man in an overcoat and carrying an umbrella. As they pass Skinny, Hildy says:

HILDY

Hi, Skinny!

Hildy greets the switchboard operators.

HILDY

Hello, Ruth. Hello, Maisie.

RUTH

Hello, Hildy.

MAISIE

Hello, Hildy.

HILDY JOHNSON

Tell me, is the lord of the universe in?

RUTH

Yes, he's in.

MAIZE

In a bad humor.

RUTH

Somebody must have stolen the crown jewel.

MAIZE

Shall we announce you?

HILDY JOHNSON

Oh, no, no. I'll blow my own horn.

Hildy goes up to Bruce.

HILDY

He's in. You should better wait here, I'll be back in ten minutes.

BRUCE BALDWIN

Even ten minutes is a long time to be away from you.

HILDY JOHNSON

What did you say?

BRUCE BALDWIN

Huh?

HILDY JOHNSON

Go on. Oh, go ahead.

BRUCE BALDWIN

Oh, I just said to you, even ten minutes is a long time
to be away from you.

HILDY JOHNSON

I heard you the first time. I like it; that's why I asked
you to say it again. I can stand being spoiled a little.
The gentleman I'm going to see did very little spoiling.

BRUCE BALDWIN

I'd like to spoil him just once. Sure you don't want me
to go in with you?

HILDY JOHNSON

Oh, no. I can handle him.

BRUCE BALDWIN

Well, if things get rough, remember I'm here.

HILDY JOHNSON

I'll come running, partner.

Hildy passes by and greets a number of people in the city room.

HILDY

Hello, Jim.

JIM

Hello.

HILDY JOHNSON

How are you?

OTHER JOURNALISTS

How are you? Hi, Hildy, welcome back. Hello, Hildy. How've you been?

HILDY JOHNSON

Good.

OTHER JOURNALISTS

Hi, Hildy.

Hildy passes by Beatrice, the lonely hearts columnist.

BEATRICE

Hello.

HILDY JOHNSON

Hello, Beatrice, how is the advice to the lovelorn?

BEATRICE

Fine. My cat just had kittens again.

HILDY JOHNSON

It's her own fault.

Hildy walks into Walter Burns' office. She knocks only once she is in. Walter Burns, managing editor of the *Morning Post*, is shaving himself with an electric razor.

LOUIE

(advising Walter on his shave)

All right, a little more around the chin bone. What do you want?

HILDY JOHNSON

Your ex-wife is here. Do you want to see her?

WALTER BURNS

Well, hello, Hildy!

HILDY JOHNSON

Hello, Walter.

LOUIE

Hi, Hildy.

HILDY JOHNSON

Oh, hello, Louie. How's the big slot machine king?

LOUIE

Oh, I ain't doing that no more. I'm retired. You know what I mean?

Duffy, the pudgy city editor with a vest and glasses, comes in.

DUFFY

So, Walter.

WALTER BURNS

I'm busy.

DUFFY

Oh, hello, Hildy.

HILDY JOHNSON

Hello, Duffy.

DUFFY

Listen.

WALTER BURNS

Get going, I'm busy.

DUFFY

I thought you ought to know that the governor didn't sign that reprieve.

WALTER BURNS

What?

DUFFY

And tomorrow morning, Earl Williams dies and makes a sucker out of us. Well, what you going to do?

WALTER BURNS

Get the governor on the phone.

DUFFY

I can't.

WALTER BURNS

Why not?

DUFFY

I can't locate him. He's out fishing.

WALTER BURNS

How many places to fish are there?

DUFFY

Well, at least two. The Atlantic and Pacific.

WALTER BURNS

All right. That simplifies it, doesn't it?

DUFFY

Oh, yeah.

WALTER BURNS

Get him on the phone.

DUFFY

And tell him what?

HILDY JOHNSON

Quiet, Duffy, he's thinking.

WALTER BURNS

Tell him if he'll reprieve Earl Williams, we'll support him for senator.

DUFFY

What?

WALTER BURNS

Tell him the Morning Post will be behind him, hook, line, and sinker.

DUFFY

But you can't do that.

WALTER BURNS

Why not?

DUFFY

Because we've been a Democratic paper for over twenty years.

WALTER BURNS

All right. After we get the reprieve, we'll be Democratic again.

DUFFY

Oh, Walter.

WALTER BURNS

Go on, Duffy. Get going. Remember the Morning Post expects every city editor to do his duty!

DUFFY

All right, all right.

Duffy leaves.

WALTER BURNS

You too, Louie, get out of here.

LOUIE

Okay, boss.

Louie leaves too.

HILDY JOHNSON

Well, Walter, I see you're still at it.

WALTER BURNS

It's the first time I ever double-crossed a governor. What can I do for you?

HILDY JOHNSON

Well, would you mind if I sat down?

WALTER BURNS

There's been a lamp burning in the window for you, honey, here.

Walter beckons her over to his lap.

HILDY JOHNSON

Oh, I jumped out that window a long time ago, Walter.

Walter lights a cigarette.

HILDY

Oh, may I have one of those?

Walter tosses the pack of cigarettes over to Hildy. She takes one.

HILDY

And the match.

Walter hands over the matches. Hildy lights up.

HILDY

Thank you.

WALTER BURNS

Well, well, how long is it?

HILDY JOHNSON

How long is what?

WALTER BURNS

You know what. How long is it since we've seen each other?

HILDY JOHNSON

Oh, well, let's see. I spent six weeks in Reno, then Bermuda—about four months, I guess. Seems like yesterday to me.

WALTER BURNS

Maybe it was yesterday. Hildy, been seeing me in your dreams?

HILDY JOHNSON

Oh no. Mama doesn't dream about you anymore, Wally, you wouldn't know the old girl now.

WALTER BURNS

Ah, yes, I would. I'd know you anytime, anyplace . . .

HILDY JOHNSON

Anywhere. You're repeating yourself, Walter. That's the speech you made the night you proposed.

WALTER BURNS

Yeah, I know that you still remember it.

HILDY JOHNSON

Of course I remember it. If I didn't remember it, I wouldn't have divorced you.

WALTER BURNS

Yeah. So I wish you hadn't done that, Hildy.

HILDY JOHNSON

Done what?

WALTER BURNS

Divorce me. Makes a fellow lose all faith in himself. Gives him, almost gives him a feeling he wasn't wanted.

HILDY JOHNSON

Oh, no. Look, junior, that's what divorces are for.

WALTER BURNS

Nonsense. You've got an old-fashioned idea divorce is something that lasts forever until death do us part. Why, divorce doesn't mean anything nowadays, Hildy, just a few words, mumbled over you by a judge. We've got something between us nothing can change.

HILDY JOHNSON

Well, I suppose you're right in a way, Walter.

WALTER BURNS

Sure I'm right.

HILDY JOHNSON

I am fond of you; you know?

WALTER BURNS

Atta girl!

HILDY JOHNSON

I often wish you weren't such a stinker.

WALTER BURNS

Latin, I suppose. You must come up and meet my mother; she'd like that kind of phrase.

HILDY JOHNSON

And why on earth did you promise not to fight the divorce and do everything you possibly could to gum up the whole works?

WALTER BURNS

Well, I meant to let you go, Hildy. But you know how it is. You never miss the water until the well runs dry.

HILDY JOHNSON

Oh, a big fat lummox like you hiring an aeroplane to write, "Hildy, don't be hasty, remember my dimple, Walter." Delayed our divorce twenty minutes while the judge went out to watch it.

WALTER BURNS

Well, I don't want to brag, but I've still got the dimple, and in the same place. Look, Hildy, I only acted like any husband who didn't want to see his home broken up.

HILDY JOHNSON

What home?

WALTER BURNS

What home? Don't you remember the home I promised you?

HILDY JOHNSON

Sure, I do. That was the one we would have right after the honeymoon.

(laughing)

Ah, honeymoon.

WALTER BURNS

Oh, was it my fault? Did I know that coal mine was going to have another cave-in? I intended to be with you on our honeymoon, Hildy, honestly, I did.

HILDY JOHNSON

All I know is that instead of two weeks in Atlantic City with my bridegroom, I spent two weeks in a coal mine with John Krupsky. You don't deny that, do you, Walter?

WALTER BURNS

Deny it? I'm proud of it. We beat the whole country on that story.

HILDY JOHNSON

Suppose we did! That isn't what I got married for. Oh, what is the good . . . Look, now look, what I came up here to tell you is that you must stop phoning me a dozen times a day, sending me twenty telegrams.

WALTER BURNS

I write a beautiful telegram, don't I? Everybody says so.

HILDY JOHNSON

Are you going to listen to what I have to say?

WALTER BURNS

Look, look, what's the use of fighting, Hildy? I'll tell you what you do. You come back to work on the paper; if we find we can't get along in a friendly fashion, we'll get married again.

HILDY JOHNSON

What?

WALTER BURNS

Certainly, I haven't any hard feelings.

HILDY JOHNSON

Oh Walter, you are wonderful in a loathsome sort of way. Now, would you please be quiet just long enough for me to tell you what I came up here to say?

WALTER BURNS

Can we have some lunch?

HILDY JOHNSON

I have a lunch date already.

WALTER BURNS

Well, break it.

He grabs her by the arm.

HILDY JOHNSON

I cannot break it. Will you take your hands off me? What are you, playing osteopath?

WALTER BURNS

Temper, temper.

HILDY JOHNSON

Oh, listen, Walter, you are no longer my husband and no longer my boss. And you're not going to be my boss.

WALTER BURNS

What's that supposed to mean?

HILDY JOHNSON

Just what I say.

WALTER BURNS

You mean you're not coming back to work on the paper?

HILDY JOHNSON

You are right, Mr. Burns, for the first time today.

WALTER BURNS

Got a better offer, huh?

HILDY JOHNSON

You bet I've got a better offer.

WALTER BURNS

All right, go on. Take it, work for somebody else. That's the gratitude I get.

HILDY JOHNSON

Oh, I wish you would stop hamming.

WALTER BURNS

When you came here five years ago, a little college girl
from a school of journalism, I took a doll-faced hick . . .

HILDY JOHNSON

Well, you wouldn't take me if I hadn't been doll-faced.

WALTER BURNS

Oh, why shouldn't I? I thought you might be a novelty.
You have a face around here a man could look at without shuddering.

HILDY JOHNSON

Listen, Walter!

WALTER BURNS

Listen, I made a great reporter out of you, Hildy, but
you won't be half as good on any other paper and you
know it. We are a team, that's what we are.

HILDY

(to block what he is saying)

La la la la la lal . . .

WALTER BURNS

You need me, and I need you, and the paper needs
both of us.

HILDY JOHNSON

Sold American!

WALTER BURNS

Oh, Lord God.

HILDY JOHNSON

Listen, Walter, please. The paper's going to have to get along without me; so are you. It just didn't work out, Walter.

WALTER BURNS

Well, it would've worked out if you'd be satisfied with just being editor and reporter, but not you. You had to marry me and spoil everything.

HILDY JOHNSON

I suppose I proposed to you!

WALTER BURNS

Well, you practically did, making goo-goo eyes with me for two years until I broke down. Oh, Walter, and I still claim I was tight the night I proposed to you. If you'd have been a gentleman, you've forgotten all about it, but not you.

HILDY JOHNSON

Why you!

She throws her purse at him. He ducks.

WALTER BURNS

You're losing your eye. You used to be able to pitch better than that.

The phone rings. Walter picks it up.

WALTER BURNS

Hello? Yeah, What, Sweeney? What can I do for you?

We see Duffy at his desk in the city room.

DUFFY

What? Wait a minute, I'm not Sweeney, I'm Duffy.

WALTER BURNS

Listen, Sweeney, you can't do that to me. Not today of all days.

DUFFY

What's the matter with you? Are you loony?

WALTER BURNS

Jumping Jehosaphat. Now listen, Sweeney, this is no time . . .

(into the phone)

Oh, all right, I suppose so. Yes. If you have to, you have to.

HILDY JOHNSON

He had to.

WALTER BURNS

How do you like that? Everything happens to me. 365 days in a year, and this has to be the day.

HILDY JOHNSON

What's the matter, Walter?

WALTER BURNS

Sweeney.

HILDY JOHNSON

Dead?

WALTER BURNS

Might just as well be the only man on the paper that can write, and he picks this day to have a baby.

HILDY JOHNSON

Well, he didn't do it on purpose, did he?

WALTER BURNS

I don't care whether he did or not. He's supposed to be covering the Earl Williams case. And where is he? Walking up and down in the hospital. Is there no sense of honor in this country?

HILDY JOHNSON

Well, haven't you got anybody else?

WALTER BURNS

No, there's nobody else on the paper that can write. This'll break me. Unless, Hildy . . .

HILDY JOHNSON

No.

WALTER BURNS

Hildy, you've got to help me out, just this once . . .

HILDY JOHNSON

Don't bother, I'll get going.

Duffy comes in but Walter sends him out immediately.

WALTER BURNS

Get out of here, Duffy, I'm busy.

(to Hildy)

This will bring us back together again. Just the way we used to be.

HILDY JOHNSON

That's just what I'm afraid of.

(mocking)

Anytime, anyplace, anywhere!

WALTER BURNS

Don't mock me. This is bigger than anything that ever happened to us. Don't do it for me, do it for the paper.

HILDY JOHNSON

Scram, Svengali.

WALTER BURNS

If you won't do it for love, how about money? Forget the other offer. I'll raise you 25 bucks a week.

HILDY JOHNSON

Listen to me, you great, big, bumble-headed baboon.

WALTER BURNS

I'll make it 35 bucks and not a cent more.

HILDY JOHNSON

Well, are you going to listen?

WALTER BURNS

Well, good grief, how much is that other paper going to pay you?

HILDY JOHNSON

There isn't any other paper.

WALTER BURNS

Oh, well, in that case, the raise is off. You go back to your old salary. How do you like that? Trying to black-jack me!

HILDY JOHNSON

I want to show you something.

The phone rings. Walter picks it up.

WALTER BURNS

I am busy.

He hangs up immediately. Hildy holds out her hand to him. She is wearing an engagement ring.

HILDY JOHNSON

It's here. It's a ring. Take a good look at it. You know what it is? It's an engagement ring. Tried to tell you right away, but you would start reminiscing. I'm getting married, Walter, and I'm also getting as far away from the newspaper business as I can get.

WALTER BURNS

What?

HILDY JOHNSON

I am through.

WALTER BURNS

You can marry all you want, Hildy, but you can't quit the newspaper business.

HILDY JOHNSON

No. Why not?

WALTER BURNS

I know you, Hildy. I know what quitting would mean to you.

HILDY JOHNSON

Well, what would it mean?

WALTER BURNS

It would kill you.

HILDY JOHNSON

You can't sell me that, Walter Burns.

WALTER BURNS

Who says I can't? You're a newspaper man.

HILDY JOHNSON

That's why I'm quitting. I want to go someplace where I can be a woman.

WALTER BURNS

You mean be a traitor?

HILDY JOHNSON

A traitor. A traitor to what?

WALTER BURNS

A traitor to journalism. You're a journalist, Hildy.

HILDY JOHNSON

A journalist. Now what does that mean? Peeking through keyholes, chasing up the fire engines, waking people up in the middle of the night to ask them if Hitler's going to start another war, stealing pictures off old ladies? I know all about reporters, Walter—a lot of daffy buttinskis running around without a nickel in their pockets. And for what? So a million hired girls, mothers, and wives will know what's going on while . . . ? Oh, what's the use? Walter, you wouldn't know what it means. I want to be a respectable woman and live a halfway normal life. Point is, I'm through.

WALTER BURNS

Where'd you meet this man?

HILDY JOHNSON

Bermuda.

WALTER BURNS

Rich, huh?

HILDY JOHNSON

He is not what you'd call rich, makes a $5,000 a year.

WALTER BURNS

What's his line?

HILDY JOHNSON

He's in the insurance business.

WALTER BURNS

Insurance business?

HILDY JOHNSON

Well, that's a good, honest business, isn't it?

WALTER BURNS

Oh, certainly it's honest, it's also adventurous, it's romantic. Listen, Hildy, I can't picture you being surrounded by policies. Policies—

HILDY JOHNSON

Well, I like it. What's more? Besides, he forgets the office when he's with me. He doesn't treat me like an errand boy either, Walter; he treats me like a woman.

WALTER BURNS

He does, does he? Mm-hmm. How did I treat you? Like a water buffalo?

HILDY JOHNSON

I don't know from water buffaloes, but I do know about him. He's kind and he's sweet and he's considerate. He wants a home and children.

WALTER BURNS

Sounds more like a guy I ought to marry. What's his name?

HILDY JOHNSON

Uh, Baldwin. Bruce Baldwin.

WALTER BURNS

Baldwin. Baldwin. Oh, I knew a Baldwin once. A horse thief from Mississippi; couldn't be the same fellow, could it?

HILDY JOHNSON

You're now talking about the man I'm marrying tomorrow.

WALTER BURNS

Tomorrow? As soon as that?

HILDY JOHNSON

Mm-hmm. Well, at last I got out what I came up here to tell you. Guess there isn't any more to the story. So long, Walter.

WALTER BURNS

So long, Hildy.

HILDY JOHNSON

And better luck to you next time.

WALTER BURNS

Thanks. Oh, Hildy.

HILDY JOHNSON

Huh?

WALTER BURNS

Uh, well, you kind of took the wind out of my sail. Look, honey, I just want to wish everything I couldn't give you.

HILDY JOHNSON

Oh, thank you, Walter.

WALTER BURNS

This other fellow, well, I'm sorry I didn't get a chance to see him. I'm more or less particular about whom my wife marries. Where is he?

HILDY JOHNSON

Oh, he's right on the job, waiting for me out there.

WALTER BURNS

Ah, do you mind if I meet him?

HILDY JOHNSON

Oh, no, Walter, it wouldn't do any good, really.

WALTER BURNS

Oh, no. You're not afraid, are you?

HILDY JOHNSON

Afraid? Of course not.

WALTER BURNS

Well, then, come on, let's see this paragon. Is he as good as you say?

HILDY JOHNSON

Oh, he's better.

WALTER BURNS

Then what does he want with you?

HILDY JOHNSON

Now you got me.

He rushes out of the office, putting on his hat.

WALTER BURNS

Oh, I am sorry, Hildy.

He lets her catch up with him.

WALTER BURNS

I suppose, Bruce, uh, what's the name?

HILDY JOHNSON

Baldwin.

WALTER BURNS

Baldwin. I suppose he opens doors for you.

HILDY JOHNSON

He does. And when he's with a lady, he takes his hat off.

WALTER BURNS

Oh, I am sorry.

He takes off his hat. But he is walking ahead of her again.

HILDY JOHNSON

And when he walks with the lady, he waits for her.

WALTER BURNS

Oh, well, in that case.

He stops and lets her precede him.

HILDY JOHNSON

Allow me.

She opens the first gate for him. He strides out and, opening the second gate, goes into the anteroom. An elderly gentleman, Mr. Davis, is sitting there; Bruce is in the background. Walter goes up to the old gentleman.

WALTER BURNS

Well, I can see right away my wife picked out the right husband for herself. How do you do, sir?

DAVIS

Must be some mistake. I'm already married.

WALTER BURNS

Already married? Oh, Hildy (*clicking his tongue*), you should have told me. Congratulations again, Mr. Baldwin.

DAVIS

Oh, no, no, my name—

Bruce Baldwin comes up from behind.

BRUCE BALDWIN

Mr. Burns.

WALTER BURNS

Excuse me, what do you want? I'm terribly busy. Just leave your card with the boy. What did you say, Mr. Baldwin?

DAVIS

My name is . . .

BRUCE BALDWIN

Mr. Burns.

WALTER BURNS

Some other time. I'm busy with Mr. Bruce Baldwin here. I didn't hear what you said, Mr. Baldwin.

DAVIS

I was going to say . . .

BRUCE BALDWIN

There is some kind of confusion.

WALTER BURNS

(to Bruce Baldwin)

Now look, what is it with you? Can't you see that . . .

BRUCE BALDWIN

I am Bruce Baldwin.

WALTER BURNS

Oh, you are Bruce Baldwin?

BRUCE BALDWIN

Yes.

WALTER BURNS

(indicating Davis)

Uh, who is he?

(to Davis)

Who are you?

DAVIS

My name's Pete Davis.

WALTER BURNS

Well, Mr. Davis, is this any concern of yours?

DAVIS

No.

WALTER BURNS

Well, from now on, I'll thank you to keep your nose out of my affairs, and don't let it happen again. That's all.

Davis sits down.

WALTER BURNS

Mr. Baldwin, I'm terribly sorry about this mistake. This is indeed a pleasure.

Walter shakes the handle of Bruce's umbrella.

WALTER BURNS

Oh, that's wrong, isn't it? Well, Bruce, you see, I thought . . . You don't mind if I call you Bruce, do you? After all, we're practically related.

BRUCE BALDWIN

Oh, not at all.

WALTER BURNS

You see my wife, that is, your wife, I mean, Hildy. Oh,
Hildy, you know, you led me to expect you were marrying a much older man.

HILDY JOHNSON

Oh, really? And what did I say that let you to expect
such . . . ?

WALTER BURNS

Oh, don't worry about it. I realize you didn't mean old
in years. You always carry an umbrella, Bruce?

BRUCE BALDWIN

Well, it looked a little cloudy this morning.

WALTER BURNS

That's right. Rubbers too, I hope.

Bruce shows Walter that he is wearing rubbers.

WALTER BURNS

Atta boy! A man ought to be prepared for any emergency.

HILDY JOHNSON

Well, Walter, I think we'd better be running along.

WALTER BURNS

Yes, we'd better be going.

BRUCE BALDWIN

Where are we going?

WALTER BURNS

I'm taking you two to lunch. Didn't you tell him, Hildy?

BRUCE BALDWIN

No, she didn't.

WALTER BURNS

Well, I guess she just wanted to surprise you, Bruce. After you. After you, Hildy.

He shows them into the elevator.

HILDY JOHNSON

You're wasting your time, Walter. It won't do you a bit of good.

WALTER BURNS

No, no. I'm glad to do it. Glad to do it.

Now Walter, Hildy, and Bruce are walking into a busy restaurant. Hildy comes up to Gus, a waiter she knows, and shakes his hand.

HILDY JOHNSON

Well, hello, Gus.

GUS

Well, don't tell me it's you, Hildy.

HILDY JOHNSON

It's none other. How have things been?

GUS

I can't complain.

WALTER BURNS

Well, I can. I'm hungry. Get me a roast beef sandwich, rare, on white bread.

Gus holds Hildy's seat as she sits down. Bruce tries to sit down next to her, but Walter gets there first. Bruce has to move to another chair, so that Walter is sitting between him and Hildy.

BRUCE BALDWIN

Oh, sorry.

WALTER BURNS

Get over there, Bruce, right here. You, Hildy?

HILDY JOHNSON

Oh, I'll have the same, I guess.

GUS

You, sir?

BRUCE BALDWIN

Yes, that's all right for me.

WALTER BURNS

Bring some mustard too, Gus.

GUS

Yes, sir.

WALTER BURNS

Huh. Well, well, well, so, uh, you two are going to get married, huh? Huh? How's it feel, Bruce?

BRUCE BALDWIN

Feels awful good. Yes, sir.

WALTER BURNS

You're getting a great little girl for yourself.

Walter and Hildy take out cigarettes. Hildy lights Walter's first.

BRUCE BALDWIN

I realize that things have been different for me ever since I met Hildy. I've never met anyone quite like her before. Everybody else I've ever known, well, you could always tell ahead of time what they're going to say or do, but Hildy is not like that. You can't tell that about her. That's nice.

WALTER BURNS

Yes. Well, you're getting something else too, Bruce. You're getting a great newspaper man.

HILDY JOHNSON

You know all this, Walter.

WALTER BURNS

One of the best I ever knew. Sorry to see her go. Darn sorry, Hildy.

HILDY JOHNSON

I'd like to believe you meant that.

WALTER BURNS

I do mean that. Listen, if you ever want to come back to the newspaper business . . .

HILDY JOHNSON

Which I won't.

WALTER BURNS

Hmm.

HILDY JOHNSON

Oh, well, in spite of everything, if I ever do, there's only one man I'd work for.

WALTER BURNS

Bet your life. I'd kill you if you ever worked for anybody else.

HILDY JOHNSON

Now, you hear that, Bruce? That's my diploma.

BRUCE BALDWIN

It must be quite a business if it's . . . Hildy, are you sure you want to quit?

HILDY JOHNSON

Uh, Bruce, what do you mean?

BRUCE BALDWIN

Well, I mean, if there's any doubt about it or if there's anything that . . . No, this is your chance to have a home and to be, like you said, a human being. I'm going to make you take that chance.

WALTER BURNS

Certainly. Why, I wouldn't let her stay. No. She deserves all this happiness, Bruce. All the things I couldn't give her. All she ever wanted was a home.

BRUCE BALDWIN

Well, I'll certainly try to give her one.

WALTER BURNS

I know you will, Bruce. Where are you going to live?

BRUCE BALDWIN

Albany.

WALTER BURNS

Albany. Huh? Got a family up there?

BRUCE BALDWIN

Oh, just my mother.

WALTER BURNS

Just your mother. Oh, you're going to live with your mother?

BRUCE BALDWIN

Well, just for the first year.

WALTER BURNS

Oh, well, that will be nice. Yes. Yes. A home with mother—in Albany too.

BRUCE BALDWIN

Mighty nice little town is Albany. They've got the state capital there, you know?

WALTER BURNS

Yeah, I know. Yeah. Well, we were there once.

(Walter bursts out laughing.)

Listen, will you ever forget the night you brought the governor back to the hotel? You see, I was in taking a bath when I came walking out without—

(Hildy pinches him under the table)

Uh, she didn't know I was in town. Well, uh, uh, Bruce, uh, how is business out there, any better?

BRUCE BALDWIN

Well, Albany's a mighty good insurance town. Most people there take it out pretty early in life.

WALTER BURNS

Yeah. Well, I can see why they would.

BRUCE BALDWIN

Statistics show that most of our policies are . . .

WALTER BURNS

You know, Bruce, I've got a feeling I ought to have taken out a little insurance. Of course, that really doesn't matter now that Hildy and I have uh, well, you know, we've, uh, does it, what does it . . . What do you think? Still at that, it might have been a good idea if we, if I, had taken out on the insurance.

BRUCE BALDWIN

Well, I honestly feel that way.

WALTER BURNS

Yeah, I think so.

BRUCE BALDWIN

I figure I'm in one business that really helps people.

WALTER BURNS

Yeah.

BRUCE BALDWIN

Of course, we don't help you much while you're alive, but afterward, that's what counts.

WALTER BURNS

Sure. I don't get it.

Hildy tries to kick Walter under the table, but kicks Gus the waiter, who has shown up at the table, instead.

WALTER BURNS

Nice going.

HILDY JOHNSON

I am so sorry. Guess my foot must have slipped.

GUS

Oh, that's all right. Uh, what would you like to drink?

WALTER BURNS

Coffee, Gus.

GUS

Shall I put some rum in the coffee? It's a nasty day.

WALTER BURNS

Sure.

HILDY JOHNSON

Oh, me too, Gus, please.

GUS

And you, sir?

BRUCE BALDWIN

Not for me, thanks.

WALTER BURNS

Go on Bruce, have a . . .

BRUCE BALDWIN

No, I have a lot to do this afternoon. I have to buy the tickets, and check the baggage.

WALTER BURNS

You'll do it tomorrow. There's plenty of time.

BRUCE BALDWIN

I can't . . .

HILDY JOHNSON

We're leaving today at four o'clock. Getting the sleeper for Albany.

WALTER BURNS

Oh, you, uh, you're leaving today at four o'clock, huh?

HILDY JOHNSON

Mm-hmm.

WALTER BURNS

That's only two hours.

HILDY JOHNSON

It doesn't give us much time at that.

BRUCE BALDWIN

No, I've got a lot to do. I ought to get . . .

Walter spills his drink and stands up abruptly.

WALTER BURNS

Look at that! Isn't that silly! All down over my front.

HILDY JOHNSON

Well, that's nothing new; here.

She hands a napkin to Walter.

WALTER BURNS

Oh, no, never mind. I'll let Gus take care of this. Hey, Gus!

Walter goes over to Gus, who starts to wipe down Walter's front.

WALTER BURNS

Gus, do something about this for me.
(whispering)
Call me to the telephone as soon as I get back to the table.

Walter slips Gus a bill.

GUS

Sure.

WALTER BURNS

Thanks, Gus. That's fine.

Walter returns to the table.

WALTER BURNS

Thanks. Sorry about that. Listen, Bruce, I, uh, let me get that straight. I must have misunderstood you. You mean you're taking a sleeper today and then getting married tomorrow?

BRUCE BALDWIN

Oh, whoa, it's not like that.

WALTER BURNS

Well, what is it like?

HILDY JOHNSON

Oh, poor Walter. He'll toss and turn all night. Perhaps you better tell him Mother is coming along too.

WALTER BURNS

Mother? Your mother kicked the bucket about . . .

BRUCE BALDWIN

No, my mother. My mother.

WALTER BURNS

Oh, your mother, oh, well, that relieves my mind.

HILDY JOHNSON

It's cruel of me to let you suffer that way. Isn't Walter sweet? Always wanting to protect me.

WALTER BURNS

Well, I admit I wasn't much of a husband, but you can
always count on me, Hildy.

BRUCE BALDWIN

I don't think she'll need you very much, Mr. Burns. I
aim to do most of the protecting myself.

Gus comes up to the table.

GUS

Mr. Burns!

WALTER BURNS

What?

GUS

Telephone.

WALTER BURNS

For me?

GUS

Yes.

WALTER BURNS

That's strange. Uh, pardon me.

Walter gets up and goes off.

BRUCE BALDWIN

You know, Hildy, he's not such a bad fellow.

HILDY JOHNSON

No, he should make some girl real happy. I'm happy.

BRUCE BALDWIN

He's not the man for you. I can see that. But I sort of like him. He's got a lot of charm.

HILDY JOHNSON

Well, it comes about naturally; his grandfather was a snake.

Walter is on the phone.

WALTER BURNS

Hello. Hello. Hey, Duffy. Listen, is there any way we could stop the four o'clock train to Albany from leaving town?

DUFFY

(off camera)

We might dynamite it.

WALTER BURNS

Could we? Oh, well, maybe we couldn't. All right, now get this, get hold of Sweeney and send him out of town on a two weeks' vacation right away. All right. Keep your shirt on. Hildy's coming back. I know she doesn't know it yet, but I promise you she's staying here. And listen, tell Louie to stick around in the office. I may need him. Goodbye.

Gus comes to the table and leaves the check.

Thanks, Gus.

Walter comes back to the table and sits down.

Uh, this is a bad business.

What's the matter, Walter?

Uh, the Earl Williams case.

Oh, yes. I've been reading about that.

It's pretty bad.

What is the lowdown on it?

Oh, it's simple, honey; poor little dope who lost his job and went berserk and shot a cop that was coming after him to quiet him down. Now they're going to hang him tomorrow.

Oh, I see.

Your paper, you've been taking his side, haven't you?

WALTER BURNS

Mm-hmm.

BRUCE BALDWIN

Well, if he was out of his mind when he did it, why doesn't the state just put him away?

WALTER BURNS

Because it happened to be a colored policeman. And you know what that means, Hildy?

HILDY JOHNSON

Mm-hmm. The colored vote's very important in this town.

WALTER BURNS

Yeah. Especially when an election is coming up in three or four days.

HILDY JOHNSON

The mayor. He'd hang his own grandmother to be reelected.

BRUCE BALDWIN

Well, you think you could just show that the man wasn't responsible?

WALTER BURNS

That's not so easy.

HILDY JOHNSON

Maybe it isn't so hard either.

WALTER BURNS

Well, what do you mean, Hildy?

HILDY JOHNSON

Don't they have to have another expert examine him before they hang him?

WALTER BURNS

Sure. A bird named Eggelhoffer is going to do it. Well, he'll say the same as all the rest.

HILDY JOHNSON

Suppose he does.

WALTER BURNS

Well, uh, what's the scheme, Hildy?

HILDY JOHNSON

Look, Walter, you get the interview with Earl Williams.

WALTER BURNS

Uh-huh.

HILDY JOHNSON

Print Eggelhoffer's statement.

WALTER BURNS

Yeah. Yeah.

HILDY JOHNSON

And right alongside of it, you know, double column.

WALTER BURNS

Uh-huh.

HILDY JOHNSON

Run your interview "Innocent man says he's sane." "Interview shows he's goofy."

WALTER BURNS

Oh, Hildy, you could do it. You can save that poor devil's life. You could. Yeah. You're going away, I'd forgotten.

HILDY JOHNSON

That's right.

BRUCE BALDWIN

How long would the interview take?

WALTER BURNS

Oh, well, about an hour for the interview, another hour to write it. That's about two hours.

BRUCE BALDWIN

Surely, we could take the six o'clock train if it'd save a man's life.

HILDY JOHNSON

No, Bruce.

(to Walter)

If you want to save Earl Williams' life, you write the interview yourself. You're still a good reporter.

WALTER BURNS

Oh, Hildy, you know I can't write that kind of thing. It takes a woman's touch; it needs that heart.

HILDY JOHNSON

Don't get poetic, Walter, get Sweeney. He's the best man you've got on the paper for that soft sister stuff.

WALTER BURNS

Poor Sweeney. Duffy just told me his wife finally had twins. Isn't that terrible? Well, Sweeney went out to celebrate. Now we can't find him anymore. So Sweeney has twins and Earl Williams gets hanged tomorrow.

HILDY JOHNSON

Now Walter, look, it isn't . . .

WALTER BURNS

(to Bruce)

Well, you argue with her. You argue with her. Otherwise you're going on a honeymoon with blood on your hands. How can you have any happiness after that? All through the years, you'll remember that a man went to the gallows because she was too selfish to wait two hours. I tell you, Bruce, Earl William's face will come between you on the train tonight and at the preacher's tomorrow and all the rest of your lives.

HILDY JOHNSON

Stop, stop, stop.

BRUCE BALDWIN

Hildy.

HILDY JOHNSON

Walter, shh!

WALTER BURNS

What? Huh?

HILDY JOHNSON

I just remembered Sweeney was only married four months ago.

Walter and Hildy burst out laughing.

WALTER BURNS

All right, Hildy, you win. I'm licked.

BRUCE BALDWIN

So Mr. Sweeney didn't have twins.

HILDY JOHNSON

No indeed. The twins were Walter's, all his.

WALTER BURNS

Oh, it was nothing. Well, come on. Let's forget it. Here, we'll start all over again. Now I'll offer you two a business proposition.

HILDY JOHNSON

We're not interested.

WALTER BURNS

(to Bruce)

Well, you'll be interested; now you are a smart young man.

HILDY JOHNSON

Don't listen to him, Bruce, I know him a little. From way back. And he never . . .

WALTER BURNS

I'm talking to him. Now look Bruce, you persuade Hildy to do the story and you can write out a nice fat insurance policy for me. What do you say to that?

BRUCE BALDWIN

Oh, no, no, no.

WALTER BURNS

Come on, Bruce.

BRUCE BALDWIN

No, I wouldn't use my wife for business purposes.

HILDY JOHNSON

Wait a minute, Bruce. Walter, how big a policy?

WALTER BURNS

Well, $25,000, $50,000.

HILDY JOHNSON

What's the commission on a hundred-thousand-dollar policy?

WALTER BURNS

Around a thousand dollars, but Hildy . . .

HILDY JOHNSON

What's wrong with a thousand dollars?

BRUCE BALDWIN

Well, I couldn't . . .

HILDY JOHNSON

We could use that money, Bruce. How long would it take to get him examined?

WALTER BURNS

Well, I could get a company doctor here in twenty minutes. But if you don't like the idea . . .

HILDY JOHNSON

You keep out of this. All right, Bruce, suppose you have Mr. Burns examined over in his office and see what they'll allow on that old carcass of his. If his . . .

WALTER BURNS

Hey, I'm better than I ever was.

HILDY JOHNSON

That's nothing to brag about. Now look Bruce, I'll go back and change and dress, and after you get the check, you phone me. I'll be in the press room at the criminal courts building. Walter?

WALTER BURNS

What?

HILDY JOHNSON

By the way, I think you better make that a certified check.

WALTER BURNS

Why do you think I am—a crook?

HILDY JOHNSON

Yes. No certified check, no story. Get me?

WALTER BURNS

It'll be certified. Want my fingerprints?

HILDY JOHNSON

No, thanks. I've still got those.

WALTER BURNS

Gus, how much do I owe you?

Walter goes off to pay. Walter helps Hildy put her coat on, somewhat awkwardly.

BRUCE BALDWIN

Oh, I'm sorry.

HILDY JOHNSON

It's all right. How much money have you got with you?

BRUCE BALDWIN

YOU KNOW. EVERYTHING WE HAVE $500.

HILDY JOHNSON

Give me the 500.

BRUCE BALDWIN

But I have to buy the tickets.

HILDY JOHNSON

I'll buy the tickets.

BRUCE BALDWIN

But I should . . .

HILDY JOHNSON

Believe me, dear, I know what I'm doing. He could get you in a crap game or something . . .

BRUCE BALDWIN

Honey, I don't gamble.

HILDY JOHNSON

I know a lot of people who never did anything before they met Walter Burns. Please, dear.

BRUCE BALDWIN

All right. Remember, it's everything we have in the world.

Bruce takes out his wallet and gives Hildy the money.

HILDY JOHNSON

I know.

WALTER BURNS

Oh, Bruce, you got change for a 10?

BRUCE BALDWIN

I just—

HILDY JOHNSON

See what I mean, don't you, Bruce?

BRUCE BALDWIN

I just gave everything I had to Hildy. All I've got left . . .

Bruce goes into his pocket and pulls out some coins. Walter hands the check to Hildy.

HILDY JOHNSON

Not me.

(indicating the check)

Sign it.

WALTER BURNS

Oh, all right.

Walter takes the coins from Bruce.

WALTER BURNS

For the waiter.

HILDY JOHNSON

Come on, Bruce.

In the press room of the criminal courts building, four reporters, Murphy, Endicott, Schwartz, and Wilson, are playing poker. Another reporter, McCue, is sitting at the phone a short distance away. They are all wearing hats except Murphy, who is wearing eyeshades and glasses. Each has a phone next to him to connect him with his newspaper's office.

WILSON

I am looking for that.

MURPHY

I am in.

ENDICOTT

I'll stay. Right?

Another phone, next to McCue rings. He answers it.

MCCUE

(answering the phone)

Wilcox 3/400.

WILSON

How many?

MURPHY

Two.

Another phone starts to ring next to McCue.

MCCUE

So take that, one of you birds. You aren't doing anything, Ernie.

The reporters playing poker ignore him.

MURPHY

I'll take two.

ENDICOTT

And one for the dealer.

BENSINGER

What's the matter with you guys, crippled or something?

(answering the second phone)

Press room. Huh? Wait a minute.

(into the first phone)

Hello, Sarge, McCue talking. Hold the line, will you?

(into the second phone)

What? Hello? No, I told you this is the press room in the criminal courts building.

Behind the poker players is another reporter, Bensinger, who is also on the phone.

BENSINGER

(into the phone)

Well, Jake, new lede on the hanging, this alienist from New York, Dr. Max J. Eggelhoffer. Eggelhoffer. Yeah. He's going to interview Williams in about half an hour in the sheriff's office.

Murphy picks up the phone next to him.

MURPHY

(into the phone)

That must be about the 10th alienist they put on Williams. If he wasn't crazy before, he would be by the time 10 of those babies got through psychoanalyzing.

(into this phone)

Give me the desk.

WILSON

Is this guy Eggelhoffer any good?

ENDICOTT

Figure it out from yourself. He's the guy they sent to Washington to interview the Brain Trust.

MURPHY

I'm in.

ENDICOTT

He said they were sane.

Another reporter, Bensinger, is sitting at a desk behind the poker game. He is on the phone.

BENSINGER

(on the phone)

Here's the situation on the eve of the hanging.

MURPHY

I'll pick up a little fudge.

(on the phone)

Uh, this is Murphy. More slop on the hanging.

BENSINGER

A double guard has been thrown around the jail, municipal buildings, railroad terminals, and elevated stations to prepare for the expected general uprising of radicals at the hour of execution.

MURPHY

(into the phone)

Uh, the sheriff has just put 200 more relatives on the payroll to protect the city from the Red Army, which is leaving Moscow in a couple of minutes.

ENDICOTT

When the real red menace shows up, the sheriff will still be crying wolf. What do you got?

                              MURPHY

                        (showing his cards)

Is that good?

                          HILDY JOHNSON

Sure. Looks good from here.

**The men look up to see Hildy standing over them. She is wear-
ing an overcoat and carrying a suitcase.**

                              MURPHY

Well, Hildy.

                             ENDICOTT

Hello, Hildy.

                              MURPHY

When did you get back?

                          HILDY JOHNSON

How are you, Ernie?

                              MCCUE

Hi, Hildy, glad to see you.

                          HILDY JOHNSON

Glad to see you.

                             ENDICOTT

Where'd you get the hat?

                          HILDY JOHNSON

I paid 12 bucks for that hat.

MURPHY

Going back to work?

HILDY JOHNSON

Uh, just a farewell appearance. I'm going into business for myself.

MCCUE

In what doing?

HILDY JOHNSON

I'm getting married tomorrow.

ALL

Why?

BENSINGER

Again? Are we invited to the wedding?

HILDY JOHNSON

Oh, I might use you for a bridesmaid, Roy.

BENSINGER

Oh.

HILDY JOHNSON

How are you, Murphy?

MURPHY

Hildy.

ENDICOTT

What are you getting married for, Hildy?

HILDY JOHNSON

None of your business.

MCCUE

You ain't fooling us, are you, Hildy?

Hildy takes out three tickets from her purse.

HILDY JOHNSON

What? Look what I've got in here three tickets to Albany on the six o'clock train tonight.

MCCUE

What do you mean three?

HILDY JOHNSON

For me and my beau, and, hats off, boys, his sweet darling mom.

MCCUE

Oh, that's nice.

ENDICOTT

What kind of marriage is that?

HILDY JOHNSON

It's going to be all right. I'm going to settle down. I'm through with the newspaper business.

ENDICOTT

Can you picture Hildy singing lullabies and hanging out didies?

MCCUE

Swapping lies over the back fence?

MURPHY

That's if she gets tired beating out rugs.

HILDY JOHNSON

TIRED OF BEATING RUGS I DON'T . . .

A bell rings repeatedly.

HILDY JOHNSON

That's in Jefferson, isn't it? Where that central school
is?

MURPHY

No school this time of day.

MCCUE

What do you care? You quit.

ENDICOTT

Hey, you said you were through.

HILDY JOHNSON

I just thought might be a good fire. That's all.

The noise of a dull thud.

HILDY JOHNSON

And what's that?

MCCUE

Just practicing for the Williams party in the morning.
You're going to miss a nice hanging, Hildy.

HILDY JOHNSON

Not interested.

McCue and Hildy go over to the window. Below they see a scaffold and policemen testing its strength by dropping a weight.

MURPHY

Tell them to pipe down.

MCCUE

(calling down)

Hey, keep quiet down there. How do you expect us to
get any work done?

POLICEMAN

Oh, shut up.

HILDY JOHNSON

Real low respect for the press around here. Say, did
anybody phone me?

BENSINGER

Not that I know of.

ENDICOTT

So, Hildy, does Walter know you're getting married?

HILDY JOHNSON

Just had lunch with him.

BENSINGER

Does he know you're quitting?

HILDY JOHNSON

Yes. I told him. Any more questions?

MURPHY

Can I deal you in, Hildy?

HILDY JOHNSON

I haven't got time. I have to do a yarn on Williams. Did he know what he was doing when he fired that gun?

MURPHY

Well, if you ask us, no. If you ask the state alienists, the answer is yes.

HILDY JOHNSON

Who is he? What's he do?

MCCUE

He was a bookkeeper. He starts in at $20 a week, and after 14 years, he gradually works himself up to $17.50. McCuskey company goes out of business and Williams loses his job.

MALE SPEAKER

Time's up.

HILDY JOHNSON

Can't get another?

MCCUE

No.

I'm in.

WILSON

And so he starts hanging around the park, listening to a lot of soapbox spellbinders, making phony speeches and begins to believe them.

ENDICOTT

And make some of his own.

SCHWARTZ

Up a dime.

WILSON

I'm in.

Back in Walter's office, he is putting his shirt and tie back on. The insurance company doctor has just finished examining him. Bruce is writing up an insurance policy on his desk.

WALTER BURNS

Anything else, doc?

INSURANCE DOC

No, that's all, Mr. Burns.

WALTER BURNS

Everything okay?

INSURANCE DOC

You have nothing to worry about.

WALTER BURNS

Good. Good. How're you doing, Bruce?

BRUCE BALDWIN

Uh, there's just one more thing, Mr. Burns.

INSURANCE DOC

Good day Mr. Burns. Mr. Baldwin.

BRUCE BALDWIN

All right, doc, thanks very much.

WALTER BURNS

Goodbye, doc.

The doctor goes out.

BRUCE BALDWIN

Who is the beneficiary?

WALTER BURNS

Uh, uh, excuse me, excuse me?

BRUCE BALDWIN

That is in case of your death, who do we pay the money to?

WALTER BURNS

Why, Hildy, of course.

BRUCE BALDWIN

Oh, I don't know. That'd make me feel pretty funny.

WALTER BURNS

Oh, no, why shouldn't I make Hildy my, uh, whatever it was?

BRUCE BALDWIN

You know, I feel I should take care of her.

WALTER BURNS

But you will take care of her, Bruce. Say that doctor is right, I'm good for a long time. Look, Bruce, this is a debt of honor with me. I was a bad husband to Hildy. She could have claimed a lot of alimony if she wanted to, but she wouldn't take any. She had it coming to her, but she was too independent.

BRUCE BALDWIN

Well, I'm independent too, you know.

WALTER BURNS

I know you are, Bruce. I know you are. But look, you just figure it this way. I'm good for, well, we'll say at least 25 years yet. Well, by that time you'll probably have made enough so the money won't mean anything to you. But suppose you haven't made good, Bruce, what about Hildy's old age? Think of Hildy. Uh, I can see her now. White head, lavender, and old lace. Can't you see her, Bruce?

BRUCE BALDWIN

Yes. Yes, I can.

WALTER BURNS

She's old, isn't she? Now, Bruce, don't you think that Hildy is entitled to spend her last remaining years without worries of money? Of course you do, Bruce.

BRUCE BALDWIN

Of course, if you put it that way . . .

WALTER BURNS

And remember, I love her too.

Duffy walks in and hears this. He frowns.

BRUCE BALDWIN

Yes, I'm beginning to realize that.

WALTER BURNS

And the beauty of it is, she'll never have to know until I've passed on.

Duffy is listening and shaking his head.

WALTER BURNS

Oh, well, maybe she'll think kindly of me after I'm gone.

Walter makes to wipe a tear from his eye and taps Bruce on the shoulder to make sure he sees it.

BRUCE BALDWIN

Jeez.

Bruce, touched, blows his nose noisily.

BRUCE BALDWIN

Make me feel like a heel coming between you.

WALTER BURNS

No, no, Bruce, you didn't come between us. It was all over for her before you came on the scene. For me . . .

DUFFY

Hey, Walter.

WALTER BURNS

It'll never be.

> *(to Duffy)*

What do you want?

DUFFY

Can I see you a minute, please?

WALTER BURNS

Excuse me, Bruce.

Walter and Duffy walk out of Walter's office.

WALTER BURNS

Did you get it?

DUFFY

Yes.

WALTER BURNS

Where is it?

DUFFY

There.

Duffy hands Walter the certified check.

WALTER BURNS

Certified?

DUFFY

Sure. But Walter, that's for $2,500.

Walter goes back into his office and hands the check to Bruce.

WALTER BURNS

Well, Bruce, here we are, certified and everything.

BRUCE BALDWIN

Certified. Gosh, I'm afraid Hildy will feel ashamed to think she hasn't trusted you, but she'll know someday.

WALTER BURNS

Oh yeah. Oh, Bruce, you promised to phone her as soon as you got the check.

BRUCE BALDWIN

Oh, yes, yes, of course.

WALTER BURNS

Get me Hildy Johnson, press room, criminal courts building. Uh, sit down, Bruce. Uh, the operator will get her for you.

BRUCE BALDWIN

Thank you.

He hands Bruce the receiver. Bruce takes the phone and sits down.

WALTER BURNS

Excuse me, will you?

Walter goes out of his office.

BRUCE BALDWIN

(into the phone)

Yes. Hello? Yes. I'll wait.

In the press room, the phone rings. Endicott picks it up.

ENDICOTT

Start hollerin'.

He hands the phone to Hildy.

HILDY JOHNSON

Thank you. Hello, Johnson speaking. Oh, hello, Bruce.

ENDICOTT

I got a dime—

MURPHY

Well, what about me? We've been playing for an hour.

HILDY JOHNSON

Take it easy, will you? Hello, Bruce. Uh, did you get the check? Is it certified?

Bruce is talking from Walter's office.

BRUCE BALDWIN

Certified and everything. I have it right in my pocket.

HILDY JOHNSON

Oh, in your pocket. That's fine. Wait a minute. Maybe it isn't so fine. Bruce, where are you?

BRUCE BALDWIN

I'm in Mr. Burns' office.

HILDY JOHNSON

Is he there? Well now, uh, look Bruce, I don't want you to carry that check around in your pocket. Well, because . . . Yes, yes, I know all that. But, uh, Bruce, uh, there's an old newspaper superstition that the first big check you get, you put in the, uh, lining of your hat. In your hat. It brings good luck.

The reporters playing poker look up at her with surprise.

MURPHY

I've been a reporter for 20 years, I've never heard that before.

HILDY JOHNSON

(to Murphy)

Neither did I.

(to Bruce)

I know it sounds silly, dear, but do it for me, please. Yes. Yes, right now.

BRUCE BALDWIN

(on the phone in Walter's office)

Just a minute.

Bruce takes the check and puts it in the lining of his hat.

BRUCE

There you are. I've done it. Anything else? Oh, yes. All right.

Walter's office has walls that are glass three-quarters of the way up. We see Walter outside. He holds up Louie (who is short) so he can see what Bruce looks like.

BRUCE

(into the phone)

Uh-huh? Yes. Yes. I'll tell him. Goodbye.

Walter walks into his office alone.

WALTER BURNS

Well, everything all right, Bruce?

BRUCE BALDWIN

Oh yes. Hildy said to tell you she'll get right to work.

WALTER BURNS

Fine.

BRUCE BALDWIN

Well, I must be going now.

Walter hands Bruce his umbrella.

WALTER BURNS

Oh, Bruce, you don't want to forget this, it might rain, you know?

BRUCE BALDWIN

Oh, thanks.

WALTER BURNS

Oh, you don't mind if I don't show you out?

BRUCE BALDWIN

No.

WALTER BURNS

I am kind of busy, I've got a lot to do.

BRUCE BALDWIN

No, thanks for everything.

WALTER BURNS

Excuse me. What'd you say?

BRUCE BALDWIN

I said thanks for everything.

WALTER BURNS

Nonsense. Don't thank me. I should thank you. So long.

BRUCE BALDWIN

So long.

They shake hands. Bruce goes out.

Hildy walks into Warden Cooley's office in the criminal courts building. Cooley is a bald, middle-aged man.

HILDY JOHNSON

Hello, Cooley.

WARDEN COOLEY

Hello, Hildy, what are you doing around here?

HILDY JOHNSON

I want an interview with Earl Williams. How about a little service?

WARDEN COOLEY

No more interviews.

HILDY JOHNSON

Why not?

WARDEN COOLEY

Sheriff's orders. Besides, the doctor is coming over. Can't do it.

She picks up a $20 bill.

HILDY JOHNSON

Say, is this your money?

WARDEN COOLEY

Why, I don't think it is.

HILDY JOHNSON

Twenty bucks.

WARDEN COOLEY

Yeah, I guess, maybe.

She hands Cooley the bill.

HILDY JOHNSON

That's what I thought. Come on, I'm in a hurry.

WARDEN COOLEY

(to a prison guard)

Hey, Joe. Open up here. Now Hildy, don't be long.

HILDY JOHNSON

I won't be long.

Hildy goes to Earl Williams' cell and talks to him through a mesh fence. He is a fragile-looking man in prison garb, with a mustache.

HILDY JOHNSON

Hello.

EARL WILLIAMS

Hello.

HILDY JOHNSON

My name's Johnson. Mind if I talk to you for a few minutes?

EARL WILLIAMS

No, I haven't anything else to do.

HILDY JOHNSON

All right.

She pulls up a chair and sits down next to the cell. Some time elapses. Hildy and Earl are talking.

EARL WILLIAMS

So you see, I couldn't plead insanity because I'm just as sane as anybody else.

HILDY JOHNSON

You didn't mean to kill that policeman.

EARL WILLIAMS

No. Well, of course not. It's against everything I've ever stood for. You know it was an accident. I'm not guilty. It's just the world.

HILDY JOHNSON

I see what you mean.

Hildy lights a cigarette and hands it to Earl through the mesh.

HILDY JOHNSON

Sorry about the lipstick, Earl. Now look, after you lost your job, uh, what did you do?

EARL WILLIAMS

I tried to find another job.

HILDY JOHNSON

I mean, how did you spend your time?

EARL WILLIAMS

Oh, I used to sit around the park, any place. Oh, I don't smoke.

He hands the cigarette back to Hildy.

HILDY JOHNSON

When you were in the park, uh, did you hear any of those speeches?

EARL WILLIAMS

You mean those fellows that talk too much?

HILDY JOHNSON

Yeah.

EARL WILLIAMS

Well I didn't pay any attention. You see, I was thinking . . .

HILDY JOHNSON

Did you hear anything?

EARL WILLIAMS

Yes.

HILDY JOHNSON

Well, that, is there anything you remember? Anything
in particular?

EARL WILLIAMS

Well, there was one fella. He uh . . .

HILDY JOHNSON

What did he talk about?

EARL WILLIAMS

He talked about production for use.

HILDY JOHNSON

Production for use.

EARL WILLIAMS

Yes, he said everything should be made use of.

HILDY JOHNSON

Makes quite a bit of sense, doesn't it?

EARL WILLIAMS

Yes, I liked him. He was a good speaker.

HILDY JOHNSON

Look, Earl, uh, when you found yourself with that gun in your hand and that policeman coming at you, what did you think about?

EARL WILLIAMS

I don't know exactly.

HILDY JOHNSON

You must have thought of something?

EARL WILLIAMS

Well . . .

HILDY JOHNSON

Could it have been production for use?

EARL WILLIAMS

I don't know. I . . .

HILDY JOHNSON

What's a gun for, Earl?

EARL WILLIAMS

A gun?

HILDY JOHNSON

Mm.

EARL WILLIAMS

Why? To shoot. Of course.

HILDY JOHNSON

Oh, and maybe that's why you used it.

EARL WILLIAMS

Maybe.

HILDY JOHNSON

Seems reasonable.

EARL WILLIAMS

Yes. Yes, it is. You see, I've never had a gun in my hand before. And that's what a gun's for, isn't it? Maybe that's why.

HILDY JOHNSON

Sure it is.

EARL WILLIAMS

Yes, that's what I thought of, production for use for . . . It's simple, isn't it?

HILDY JOHNSON

Very simple, isn't it?

EARL WILLIAMS

There's nothing crazy about that, is there?

HILDY JOHNSON

No. Nothing at all.

EARL WILLIAMS

You'll write about that in your paper, won't you?

HILDY JOHNSON

You bet I will. Who sent you the roses?

There is a bunch of roses in Earl Williams' cell.

EARL WILLIAMS

Miss Mollie Malloy. She's a wonderful person.

HILDY JOHNSON

You have a picture?

They look at a picture of Molly that is hanging in the cell.

EARL WILLIAMS

Yes, she's beautiful, isn't she?

HILDY JOHNSON

Indeed.

WARDEN COOLEY

Time is up, Hildy.

HILDY JOHNSON

All right. I guess that's all.

EARL WILLIAMS

I like talking to you. Goodbye, Miss Johnson.

HILDY JOHNSON

Goodbye, Earl. Good luck.

Hildy goes out.

In the press room of the criminal courts building, the poker game is still going on.

ENDICOTT

Three ladies.

WILSON

I wonder what the Post is going to do without Hildy.

SCHWARTZ

You suppose Walter Burns is ever going to let her go?

MURPHY

I don't know.

ENDICOTT

You remember what he did to Bill Fenton when he wanted to go to Hollywood. Had him thrown in jail for arson.

MURPHY

Forgery.

ENDICOTT

Is that it?

MURPHY

Yeah. Give me some change.

WILSON

Hey, Mac? You stairway Sam.

McCue is still at his phone on the desk.

MCCUE

Huh?

WILSON

Would you mind turning on some lights?

MCCUE

Sure.

MURPHY

I can't see anything in this place.

MCCUE

Hey, who's this guy Hildy is going to marry?

SCHWARTZ

I don't know, Bruce something.

SCHWARTZ

I give the marriage six months.

ENDICOTT

Why?

SCHWARTZ

Because she wouldn't be able to stay away from the paper any longer than that. Did you see her when that bell went off?

• 83 •

MURPHY

I thought it must be pretty nice to be able to walk out
of a place and quit.

SCHWARTZ

I bet.

WILSON

Yeah. I had a publicity job offered to me last year.
Should have taken it.

ENDICOTT

I thought I'd like a job on the side.

MURPHY

Desk and a stenographer. I wouldn't mind a nice big
blonde, with brown eyes . . .

SCHWARTZ

I bet you ten to one, it don't last six months. She's just
like us and we wouldn't be sticking around waiting for
that guy to be . . .

Mollie Malloy walks into the press room.

MCCUE

Well, well, Miss Mollie Malloy.

WILSON

Hello, Mollie.

ENDICOTT

Mollie.

WILSON

Mollie, how's tricks?

MOLLIE MOLLOY

I've been looking for you tramps.

MURPHY

Didn't you call on Williams?

MALE SPEAKER

He's right across the courtyard.

MALE SPEAKER

Better hurry up.

ENDICOTT

Nice bunch of roses you sent to Earl. What do you want done with them tomorrow morning?

MOLLIE MALLOY

A lot of wise guys, ain't you?

SCHWARTZ

You're breaking up the game, Mollie, what do you want?

MOLLIE MALLOY

I came to . . .

Hildy walks into the press room behind Mollie. She takes a piece of paper and puts it into a typewriter.

MOLLIE MALLOY

I came to tell you what I think of you, all of you.

MURPHY

Keep your shirt on.

MOLLIE MALLOY

If you was worth breaking my nails on, I'd tear your face wide open.

MURPHY

What are you sore about, sweetheart? Wasn't that a swell story we gave you?

ENDICOTT

What do you want?

MOLLIE MALLOY

You crumbs have been making a fool out of me long enough. I never said I loved Earl Williams and was willing to marry him on the gallows. You made that up about my being his soul mate and having a love nest with him.

WILSON

Well, you did, didn't you?

ENDICOTT

You've been sticking around that crook ever since they threw him in the death house.

MOLLIE MALLOY

That's a lie.

SCHWARTZ

Everybody knows you're his girlfriend.

MOLLIE MALLOY

I met Mr. Williams just once in my life.

SCHWARTZ

(to the other players)

How many?

MURPHY

Two.

MOLLIE MALLOY

When he was wandering around in the rain without his hat and coat on like a sick dog. The day before the shooting.

ENDICOTT

Give me one.

MOLLIE MALLOY

I went up to him like any human being would. And I asked him what was the matter, and he told me about being fired after being on the same job for fourteen years.

SCHWARTZ

Who bets?

WILSON

Bet 20 cents.

MOLLIE MALLOY

And I brought him up to my room because it was warm there.

ENDICOTT

Oh, put it on a phonograph.

Off to the side, Hildy is typing rapidly.

MOLLIE MALLOY

Oh, listen to me, please. I tell you he just sat there talking to me all night. He never once laid a hand on me. And in the morning, he went away, and I never saw him again until that day of the trial. Sure, I was his witness.

MURPHY

And what a witness.

MOLLIE MALLOY

That's why you're persecuting me because Earl Williams treated me decently and not like an animal.

MURPHY

Quiet down. This is the press room, we're busy.

WILSON

Why don't you go see your boyfriend?

MCCUE

Yeah, he's got a nice room.

ENDICOTT

He won't have it long. He left a call for 700 a.m.

MOLLIE MALLOY

I still wonder why a bolt of lightning from God don't come strike you all dead.

• 88 •

We hear the thud from the gallows downstairs. Mollie runs to the window and sees it.

MOLLIE MALLOY

What's that?

SCHWARTZ

They're fixing up a pain in the neck for your boyfriend.

MOLLIE MALLOY

Shame on you. Shame on you. A poor little fellow that never meant nobody no harm, sitting there this minute with the angel of death beside him and you cracking jokes.

Murphy gets up and grabs Molly by the arm.

MURPHY

All right now, take your things and get out of here. Come on.

MOLLIE MALLOY

Take your hands off me.

Hildy gets up and takes Molly by the arm.

HILDY JOHNSON

Come on, Mollie. Let's get out of here.

MOLLIE MALLOY

They are inhuman!

HILDY JOHNSON

I know they're newspapermen.

MOLLIE MALLOY

All they've been doing is lying. All they've been doing
is writing lies.

HILDY JOHNSON

Come on, Mollie.

MOLLIE MALLOY

Why won't they listen to me? Why won't they listen to
me?

Hildy leads Mollie out. The newspapermen are silent, feeling
guilty for the way they have treated Mollie. Murphy, standing,
takes some change out of his pocket and throws it on the floor
in frustration.

The phone rings. Endicott answers.

ENDICOTT

Hello. Who? Hildy Johnson? Hang on. She'll be back
in a minute.

MURPHY

You guys want to turn in the cards?

WILSON

What's the use? I can't win anyway.

The reporters shuffle around dejectedly. Hildy reappears in
the press room.

HILDY JOHNSON

Gentlemen of the press.

ENDICOTT

Hildy, phone for you.

Hildy picks up the phone.

HILDY JOHNSON

Hello? Oh, hello, Bruce. Oh? Where are you? You're where? Well, how did that happen? Never mind. Never mind. I'll be right down.

She grabs her purse and runs out of the room, accidentally kicking the shin of Sheriff Hartwell, who is entering.

HILDY JOHNSON

Oh, I'm sorry, honey. Sorry.

The sheriff hops around on one leg, in pain.

SHERIFF

Ooh! Ooh!

WILSON

Hi, Sheriff. How you doing?

SHERIFF HARTWELL

My shin, my back! What's going on around here?

WILSON

Bruce was in trouble.

ENDICOTT

Mama lioness goes to defend cub.

WILSON

Man forgets hanky. Mama goes to wipe nose.

SCHWARTZ

I still give that marriage six months.

SHERIFF HARTWELL

I don't know what you fellas are talking about.

WILSON

What do you want, Pete?

SHERIFF HARTWELL

Oh, uh, I've got the tickets for the hanging here, boys.

MURPHY

Pete. Pete.

SHERIFF HARTWELL

Huh?

MURPHY

Pete. Why can't you hang this guy at five o'clock instead of seven?

BENSINGER

Sure. It won't hurt you, and we can make the city edition.

SHERIFF HARTWELL

Oh, well, no, that's, that's kind of raw, Roy. After all, I can't hang a man in his sleep just to please the newspaper.

WILSON

No, but you can reprieve him twice so the hanging is three days before election, can't you?

ENDICOTT

You can run on a law and order ticket. You can do that, all right.

SHERIFF HARTWELL

Honestly, boys, I had absolutely nothing to do with those reprieves.

MCCUE

Yeah. How do we know there won't be another reprieve tonight?

MURPHY

What if this Eggelhoffer finds Williams insane?

SHERIFF HARTWELL

Well, he won't find him insane, because he isn't. He's just as sane as I am. Now be serious, boys. After all, this is a hanging, and it's going to go according to schedule, seven o'clock in the morning, and not a minute earlier. After all, there's such a thing as being humane, you know?

BENSINGER

All right, Pinky, when you want a favor . . .

SHERIFF HARTWELL

And please don't call me Pinky.

BENSINGER

Why is that?

SHERIFF HARTWELL

Because I got a name, see? And its Peter B. Hartwell.

MCCUE

What's the B for?

ENDICOTT

Bull.

Bruce is in a jail cell. HIldy goes up to him. Mike, the jailer, is there as well.

BRUCE BALDWIN

But I'm innocent. I didn't do anything. I never stole a watch in my . . .

HILDY JOHNSON

I know you didn't, Bruce. I know you didn't.
(to the guard)
All right, Mike, come on, let him out.

MIKE

I can't, Hildy, he's accused of stealing a watch, and they found the watch on him.

BRUCE BALDWIN

But I never stole . . .

HILDY JOHNSON

Please, Bruce. And who accused him? Diamond Louie, the biggest crook in town.

MIKE

No, it's no good, Hildy.

HILDY JOHNSON

Now don't Hildy me. Are you going to let him out or aren't you?

MIKE

No.

BRUCE BALDWIN

I never stole . . .

HILDY JOHNSON

Oh, Bruce, please.

(to Mike)

All right, you're not. Well, perhaps you better read the Post in the morning.

Next we see Hildy and Bruce in the back of a taxi.

BRUCE BALDWIN

I can't imagine who'd do a thing like that to me. I can't think of any enemies I have.

HILDY JOHNSON

I'm sure you haven't any, Bruce. Have you got the check?

BRUCE BALDWIN

Oh, yes, I have it right here.

He takes the check out of his hat and gives it to Hildy.

BRUCE BALDWIN

That's a funny superstition you newspaper people have.

HILDY JOHNSON

It is, isn't it?

BRUCE BALDWIN

About being arrested at first I thought maybe Walter Burns might have something to do with it, but then of course I realized he couldn't have.

HILDY JOHNSON

Why?

BRUCE BALDWIN

Well, he's a very nice fellow, Hildy.

HILDY JOHNSON

Oh?

BRUCE BALDWIN

Oh, yes. I found that out.

Bruce searches through his pockets but cannot find his wallet.

HILDY JOHNSON

What's the matter?

BRUCE BALDWIN

I've lost my wallet.

HILDY JOHNSON

Yes. Uh, well, Bruce, never mind, I have the money. You better give me the check too.

BRUCE BALDWIN

And that picture of us in Bermuda.

HILDY JOHNSON

Don't bother, Bruce. You'll find lots of things missing.

Hildy is getting out of the cab and closing the door. Bruce is about to get out.

HILDY

No, Bruce, dear, you wait here. I'm not taking any more chances. I'll be down in three minutes. We're taking the next train.

In the press room, Wilson is reading aloud Hildy's copy, which is still in the typewriter.

MCCUE

"And so into this little tortured mind came the idea that that gun had been produced for use and use it, he did. But the state has a production for use plan too. It has a gallows. And at 700 a.m., unless a miracle occurs, that gallows will be used to separate the soul of Earl Williams from his body, and out of Mollie Malloy's life will go the one kindly soul she ever knew." That's as far as she got. Boy, I ask you guys, can that girl write an interview?

WILSON

She'll do until somebody else comes along.

BENSINGER

I don't think it's very ethical reading other people's stuff.

ENDICOTT

Where do you get that ethics stuff? You're the only one who will swipe any of it.

SCHWARTZ

Well, I still say that anybody that can write like that ain't going to give it up permanently, much less for a guy in the insurance business. Now I give that marriage three months and I'm laying three to one. Any takers?

Hildy comes in the room suddenly.

HILDY JOHNSON

I'll take that bet. It's getting so a girl can't leave a room without being discussed by a bunch of old ladies.

Hildy picks up a phone.

HILDY JOHNSON

Hello? Post, uh, get me Walter Burns, will you, please?

WILSON

Oh, don't get sore, Hildy. We were only saying a swell reporter like you wouldn't quit so easy.

HILDY JOHNSON

(to the phone)

Uh, this is Hildy Johnson.

Oh, I can quit, all right. Without a single quiver. I'm going to live like a human being. Not like you chimps.

Is that you, Walter? Oh, I've got some news for you. Yes, yes, I got the interview all right. But I've got some more important news, and perhaps you'd better get a pencil and take it down. All ready? Now get this, you double-crossing chimpanzee. There ain't going to be any interview, and there ain't going to be any story. And that certified check of yours is leaving with me in twenty minutes. I wouldn't cover the burning of Rome for you if they were just lighting it up. If I ever lay my two eyes on you again, I'm going to walk right up to you and hammer on that monkey skull of yours till it rings like a Chinese gong. Oh, so you don't know why I'm angry with you? Well, perhaps you better get Louie to tell you the story of his watch. And there's just one other little thing I want you to listen to.

She rushes over to her desk, takes her story, and rips it up next to the phone receiver.

HILDY JOHNSON

Did you hear that? That's the story I just wrote. Yes. Yes. I know we had a bargain. I just said I'd write it; I didn't say I wouldn't tear it up. It's all in little pieces now, Walter, and I hope to do the same for you someday.

She hangs up and puts on her coat.

HILDY JOHNSON

And that, my friends, this is my farewell to the news paper game. I'm going to be a woman, not a news getting machine. I'm going to have babies and take care of them, give them cod liver oil, and watch their teeth grow. And oh, dear, if I ever see one of them look at a newspaper again, I'm going to brain them. Where's my hat?

She finds her hat and puts it on. The phone rings again.

WILSON

Hello? Well, Mr. Burns. Yes, she's still here.

HILDY JOHNSON

(into the phone)

Yes. And another thing I want . . .

She yanks the phone from its wire and throws it down in frustration. The newsmen watch aghast.

HILDY JOHNSON

Oh, where is my hat . . .

She touches her hat on her head.

HILDY JOHNSON

Oh, there it is.

The interrogation room. Dr. Eggleshoffer is standing over Earl Williams, who is sitting down. Sheriff Hartwell rushes in. Dr. Eggleshoffer is polishing his eyeglasses.

SHERIFF HARTWELL

Hello, Doctor. Sorry to be late.

DR. EGGELHOFFER

That's quite all right.

SHERIFF HARTWELL

These boys in the newspapers, they take up so much of my time. You know, they wanted me to hang Williams at their convenience. Oh, hello, Earl.

DR. EGGELHOFFER

These newspapers, what they did to me in Chicago.

SHERIFF HARTWELL

I quite believe you.

DR. EGGELHOFFER

Always after me for an interview.

SHERIFF HARTWELL

Yes, me too.

DR. EGGELHOFFER

Of course, I did rather promise to make them some sort of statement when I finished here. You don't mind, do you?

SHERIFF HARTWELL

Uh, well, that's hardly ethical, doctor. You see, all statements are supposed to come from me.

DR. EGGELHOFFER

Well, uh, what do you say to giving them some sort of joint interview? I can discuss some of the psychological aspects of the case, and you . . .

SHERIFF HARTWELL

And you mean we'd have our pictures taken together?

DR. EGGELHOFFER

Yes. Yes. Shaking hands.

SHERIFF HARTWELL

Splendid idea.

DR. EGGELHOFFER

Of course, I don't take a very good picture.

SHERIFF HARTWELL

Oh, that doesn't matter, doctor. The publicity is the main thing.

Earl Williams, watching this, shakes his head in disgust.

EARL WILLIAMS

Doctor, I'm getting awful tired. Can I go back to jail again?

DR. EGGELHOFFER

Oh, I'm awfully sorry. I forgot you were there. No, Mr. Williams, we've some other questions for you. Sheriff, do you mind extinguishing the light, please?

SHERIFF HARTWELL

Of course, doctor, certainly, certainly.

The sheriff turns off the light.

DR. EGGELHOFFER

Going to help a lot with what we have to do over here. Now, let me see. Mr. Williams, you know, of course, that you're going to be executed. Now who do you feel is responsible for that?

EARL WILLIAMS

I'm innocent. It wasn't my fault.

Back in the criminal court newsroom, Hildy is shaking hands with the newsmen to wish them farewell.

HILDY JOHNSON

Bye, Murphy.

MURPHY

Send us a postcard.

HILDY JOHNSON

That I'll do.

BENSINGER

Goodbye, Hildy.

MURPHY

When will we see you again, Johnson?

HILDY JOHNSON

Next time you see me, I shall be riding in a Rolls-Royce, giving interviews on success. So long, you wage slaves. Oh, and when you're crawling up fire escapes and getting kicked out of front doors, and eating Christmas dinners in one-arm joints, don't forget your pal, Hildy Johnson. And when the road beyond, the bulls and the . . .

She is interrupted by a terrific fusillade of shots in courtyard. A roar of excited voices comes up. For a second, everyone is motionless. There is another volley. All the reporters rush to the window.

Below we see Earl Williams fleeing from the courtyard, police running out after him.

ENDICOTT

Look out! It's a jailbreak.

MURPHY

What's the matter? What happened?

A couple of stray shots hit one of the windows of the press room.

MURPHY

Hey, watch where you're aiming, will you?

POLICEMAN

(off camera)

Not today.

ENDICOTT

Who got away? Who was it?

POLICEMAN

(off camera)

Earl Williams.

The newsmen rush to their phones. A quick montage of reporters at their various phones follows: "Gimme desk!" "Flash!" "Earl Williams just escaped!" "Don't know yet—call you back," etc., are shouted into the phones by the reporters.

WILSON

Hello! Hello!! Hurry up. Hurry up. This important.

ENDICOTT

Give me the desk line.

BENSINGER

Earl Williams just escaped.

MCCUE

Jailbreak.

MURPHY

He went over the wall.

ENDICOTT

I don't know anything.

After each man communicates with his paper, he dashes out the door Hildy watches them all run out. She takes off her coat and rushes to the phone.

HILDY JOHNSON

(into the phone)

Hello, Post, get me Walter Burns quick, it's Hildy Johnson. Walter! Walter, Hildy. Williams just escaped from the county jail. Yeah, yeah, yeah. Don't worry, I'm on the job.

She runs out of the newsroom.

In the courtyard, sirens ring, squad cars and motorcycles rush out, and policemen scurry around with rifles. Hildy, standing on the side, calls out:

HILDY JOHNSON

Hey, Cooley!

She rushes off the sidewalk and is nearly hit by a speeding motorcycle. She is running after Cooley. Cooley, seeing her, runs away. Finally she catches up with him and tackles him to the ground. She sits on him.

HILDY JOHNSON

Cooley! I want to talk to you.

Back at the newsroom, all of the newsmen's phones are ringing, but the room is empty. Endicott comes rushing in and picks up a phone.

ENDICOTT

(into the phone)

This is Endicott. Give me rewrite.

Endicott picks up another phone, which is ringing.

ENDICOTT

(into the second phone)

He ain't here.

Endicott hangs up the first phone.

ENDICOTT

(into the first phone)

Hello, Gil, here's the situation now, you ready? Williams was taken over to the sheriff's private office to be examined by this Professor Eggelhoffer. And in a few minutes, he shot his way out. No, nobody knows where he got the gun. He went upstairs into the infirmary and got out through the skylight. He must have slid down the rainpipe to the street. No, nobody knows where he got it. If they do, they won't talk.

Murphy rushes in to his phone.

MURPHY

(into the second phone)

Hello, sweetheart, give me the desk.

ENDICOTT

(into the phone)

Crime Commission offers $10,000 reward for Williams' capture.

MURPHY

(into the phone)

Murphy talking. No clue yet as to Williams' where-abouts.

ENDICOTT

Okay.

Endicott hangs up and rushes out of the room.

MURPHY

(into the phone)

No, no. Here's a little feature, though. There's been an accident about a tear bomb. Yeah. Tear bomb. Tear bomb. Criminals cry for it.

Sheriff Hartwell rushes in, along with Wilson. Wilson goes to his desk.

SHERIFF HARTWELL

I don't know.

MURPHY

(into the phone)

A tear bomb went off unexpectedly in the hands of Sheriff Hartwell's bombing squad.

SHERIFF HARTWELL

(to Murphy)

What went off?

MURPHY

(into the phone)

The following deputies were rushed to the hospital.

SHERIFF HARTWELL

(to Murphy)

What a fine friend you are!

MURPHY

(into the phone)

Their names are Mervin D. Wilkerson. The mayor's brother-in-law.

SHERIFF HARTWELL

After all I've done for you!

MURPHY

(into the phone)

Howard Schuster, the sheriff's uncle, on his mother's side.

Wilson comes in and starts talking on his phone.

WILSON

(into his phone)

Hello, Jim. Highlights from Sheriff Hartwell's manhunt.

MURPHY

(into his phone)

William Mayfield, the sheriff's landlord, and Lester Winthrop, who married the sheriff's niece. You remember the very homely thing.

WILSON

(into his phone)

All right, you ready?

MURPHY

(into his phone)

Call you back.

WILAON

(into his phone)

Mrs. William Mays, age fifty-five, scrub lady, while scrubbing the eighth floor of the commerce building, was shot in the left leg by one of Sheriff Hartwell's deputies.

SHERIFF HARTWELL

Look, I . . .

Shots fired. McCue rushes in.

MURPHY

There goes another scrub lady.

• 109 •

WILSON

It was only a flesh wound; they took her to the hospital. Call you back.

Wilson hangs up and runs out. McCue picks up his phone.

MCCUE

(into his phone)

McCue speaking. Give me the desk.

WILSON

Hey mate, I need to how he escaped.

MCCUE

Maybe the sheriff let him out so Williams could vote
for him.

Sheriff Hartwell leaves in disgust.

WILSON

(into the phone)

A man answering description of Earl Williams was
seen boarding a southbound . . . Call you back.

(seeing Hildy)

Thought you'd gone.

HILDY JOHNSON

I thought so too.

The other reporters rush out. Hildy, alone in the press room,
picks up a phone.

HILDY JOHNSON

(into the phone)

Get me Walter Burns, quick. Walter, Walter, listen, I've got the whole story on how Williams got that gun and escaped, and I got it exclusive. Yeah, yeah, that's right. And it's a pip. It cost me 450 bucks to tear it out of Cooley.

WALTER BURNS

(on the phone in his office)

Never mind that. What's the story?

HILDY JOHNSON

Well, just a minute and I'll give you the story. But I'm telling you, first I had to give him all the money I had on me, and it wasn't exactly mine. Well, it's Bruce's money, and I want it back.

WALTER BURNS

Bruce's money? Sure, sure, sure. You'll get it. Now, what's the story? I'll send the money right down to you. I swear it on my mother's grave.

HILDY JOHNSON

All right. He says . . . Wait a minute, your mother's alive.

WALTER BURNS

My grandmother's grave. Don't be technical, Hildy. What's the story?

HILDY JOHNSON

Well, you get that money down here. All right. All right. Here's your story. It's the jailbreak of your dreams. It seems this expert, Dr. Eggelhoffer, the profound thinker from New York, was giving Williams a final sanity test in the sheriff's office. You know, sticking a lot of pins in him so that he could get his reflexes. Well, he decided to reenact the crime exactly as it was taking place in order to study Williams's powers of coordination. Well, I'm coming to it! Of course, he had to have a gun to reenact the crime with, and who do you suppose supplied it? Peter B. Hartwell, B for Brains.

WALTER BURNS

No kidding.

HILDY JOHNSON

I tell you I'm not kidding. I'm not good enough to make this one up. Well, the sheriff gave his gun to the professor, and the professor gave it to Earl, and Earl shot the professor, right in the classified ad. No, head. Isn't it perfect? If the sheriff had rolled out a red carpet and handed Earl Williams an umbrella, it couldn't have been more ideal. Who? Oh no, no, Eggelhoffer wasn't badly hurt. They took him to the county hospital, where they're awfully afraid he'll recover.

WALTER BURNS

Oh, that's great work, Hildy. Huh? Oh, stop worrying about the money. I'll see you get it in 15 minutes.

HILDY JOHNSON

Well, I better get it in 15 minutes. Bruce is downstairs waiting in a taxicab for me, and we're in a hurry.

Evangeline (Angie), a sultry but disreputable-looking blonde in a black suit, and Diamond Louie are in Walter's office.

WALTER BURNS

(into the phone)

Hold on a minute.

(to Evangeline)

Hey Angie, come here. There's a guy waiting in a taxi in front of the criminal courts building. His name is Bruce Baldwin.

EVANGELINE

What does he look like?

WALTER BURNS

He looks like, um, that fellow in the movies. You know, Ralph Bellamy.

EVANGELINE

Oh, him.

WALTER BURNS

Can you handle it?

EVANGELINE

I've never flopped on you yet, have I?

WALTER BURNS

Come on, get going. You only got about two minutes. All right. Yes, dear, I'm sorry to keep you waiting. How much was it again? $450? Hold on just a second.

WALTER BURNS

(covering the receiver)

Louie, come here, I need $450 worth of counterfeit money.

LOUIE

You can't carry that much, boss.

WALTER BURNS

No, just the 450 counterfeit. Where can I get it?

LOUIE

Oh, I got that on me.

WALTER BURNS

Well, take it over to Hildy.

(into the phone)

Hello, it's coming right over. Yeah, I'm sending it over with Louie. Thanks for your story, dear. And good luck on your honeymoon.

HILDY JOHNSON

Yeah, no, never mind the thanks. Just see that money gets here.

In the newsroom, Hildy hangs up the phone. McCue comes in.

MCCUE

Oh, Hildy, you still here?

HILDY JOHNSON

No, I'm in Niagara Falls.

McCue picks up his phone.

MCCUE

McCue speaking, I got a good feature for you on the manhunt. Ready? Mrs. Phoebe de Wall, of 61 and a half South State Street, colored, gave birth to a pickaninny in a patrol wagon with Sheriff Hartwell's special rifle squad acting as nurses. Phoebe was walking along the street when . . . That's right. Yeah. So they coaxed her into the patrol wagon and started a race with the stork. When the pickaninny was born, the rifle squad examined him carefully to see if it was Earl Williams. Well, they knew he was hiding somewhere. They named the kid Peter Hartwell de Wall, after the sheriff. Yeah, they all chipped in and sent . . .

Hildy answers her phone in the newsroom.

HILDY JOHNSON

(into the phone)

Bruce, I thought you were downstairs in the . . .

MCCUE

(into his phone)

Here's another feature.

HILDY JOHNSON

Uh? Arrested again? What for this time?

Bruce is in the police station, with a couple of policemen and an indignant Evangeline watching.

BRUCE BALDWIN

Oh, well, they called it mashing. No, I didn't, Hildy. I was sitting right in the taxi where you left me, and the young lady seemed to have a dizzy spell, and I just . . . Uh? Well, uh, she's kind of, huh? Yes, she's a blonde. Yes, very blonde.

HILDY JOHNSON

(into the phone)

Never mind. I know how it happened. Just a minute.

In the newsroom, Hildy rushes over to another phone.

HILDY JOHNSON

(into the phone)

Get me Walter Burns. Hildy Johnson.

Hildy rushes back to the first phone.

HILDY JOHNSON

Bruce, where are you? Twenty-seventh precinct? Hold on a minute, will you?

Hildy rushes back to the second phone.

HILDY JOHNSON

(into the phone)

Walter, you . . . Well, he was there a minute ago, but I . . . double-crossing

(into the first phone)

Hello? No, not you, Bruce, I can't get there right away. What about twenty minutes? But you see, I have to wait here for the . . . Uh, I'll tell you when I see you. If I ever have my two hands against Walter Burns, I will tear him wide . . .

McCue and Endicott come into the newsroom.

MCCUE

Hold a minute. Anything I can do to help, Hildy?

HILDY JOHNSON

How much money do you have on you, mate?

MCCUE

Sorry, 64 cents. You're welcome to it.

HILDY JOHNSON

Thanks. You better buy an annuity.

MCCUE

(into a phone)

What's that, Emo? No, I can't give you an official statement.

The Mayor walks into the newsroom.

MCCUE

No. Wait a minute, here's the Mayor. Maybe he'll give us one. How about a statement, Mayor?

MAYOR

Don't question me now, please, I've got all on my mind.

MCCUE

His honor won't say anything.

MAYOR

Have you seen Sheriff Hartwell?

ENDICOTT

It's hard to tell, your honor, you see, there's so many cockroaches around here.

MURPHY

Whoa. Wait a minute. Wait a minute. How about a statement, your honor?

MCCUE

Sure. We go to press in twenty minutes.

MAYOR

I can't help that. I've nothing to say. Not at this time.

ENDICOTT

Uh, just a moment, please. What do you know about the escape?

MCCUE

How did he get out?

MURPHY

Where did he get the gun?

MAYOR

Wait a minute, boys, not so fast.

MCCUE

Well, give us a statement on the election then.

MURPHY

What effect will all this have on the voters?

MAYOR

None whatsoever. How can an unavoidable misfortune like this have any influence on the upright citizens of our fair city?

ENDICOTT

Mr. Mayor, please, is there a red menace or ain't there?

MCCUE

How did Williams get out of that rubber jail of yours?

MURPHY

You understand, you picked out somebody to be responsible.

ENDICOTT

Is there any truth in the report that you're on Stalin's payroll?

MCCUE

Yeah, this senator claimed you sleep in red underwear.

MAYOR

Never mind the junk. Don't forget I'm the mayor of this town.

MURPHY

Oh, hey, come here.

Sheriff Hartwell and Endicott come into the room.

MAYOR

Hartwell, I want to see you.

MURPHY

How did he get away?

MCCUE

Where did he get the gun?

BENSINGER

Hi, your Honor. Any statement on the red uprising tomorrow?

MAYOR

What red uprising?

SHERIFF HARTWELL

There'll be no red uprising.

MCCUE

(into the phone)

The governor says the situation calls for the militia. Give me rewrite.

MAYOR

You can quote me as saying anything the governor says is a tissue of lies.

SHERIFF HARTWELL

Yes.

MCCUE

Hello, Jake, here's a red-hot statement from the governor. He claims the Mayor and the Sheriff have shown themselves to be a couple of eight-year-olds playing with fire. Yeah. You can quote him as follows "It is a lucky thing for the city that next Tuesday is election day as the citizens will thus be saved the expense of impeaching the Mayor and the Sheriff." That's all, I'll call you back. Thanks. Nice to have seen you, Mayor.

McCue walks out. Sheriff Hartwell tries to follow.

SHERIFF HARTWELL

Excuse me, boys, I've got so much . . .

MURPHY

Wait a minute. Who engineered this?

ENDICOTT

Was it the Reds?

SHERIFF HARTWELL

No.

MCCUE

Who was it, you?

SHERIFF HARTWELL

Me? No, just a minute and I'll tell you. I've got him located.

MURPHY

Oh, Williams?

MCCUE

Where is he?

SHERIFF HARTWELL

Out on Center Street, where he used to live. I just got a tip.

MURPHY

But why didn't you say so?

SHERIFF HARTWELL

The rifle squad's just going out. You'll be able to catch him if you hurry. Please, look, I've got so much to do.

They all go out of the newsroom. In the corridor, Sheriff Hartwell is talking to the Mayor, who is walking rapidly away.

SHERIFF HARTWELL

Huh? See here, Fred . . .

MAYOR

Pete, you're through.

SHERIFF HARTWELL

Through? What do you mean, I'm through?

MAYOR

I mean I'm scratching your name off the ticket next to me. I'm running Sherman in your place. Reform the red!

The Mayor and the Sheriff go into the Sheriff's office.

SHERIFF HARTWELL

Yeah, but Fred . . .

MAYOR

Williams is no red, and you know it.

SHERIFF HARTWELL

But there are a lot of communistic sympathizers around. And I thought that if I got a slogan like that, I could . . .

MAYOR

But that's got nothing to do with this case. Do you realize there are 200,000 votes that stick, and if Earl Williams don't hang, we're going to lose?

SHERIFF HARTWELL

We're going to hang him. Come on. He can't get away.

MAYOR

What do you mean he can't get away? He did get away, didn't he?

Joe Pettibone, a plump, mild-mannered, mustachioed man in a bowler and a three-piece suit, comes in carrying an umbrella and a letter.

SHERIFF HARTWELL

What do you want?

JOE PETTIBONE

Are you Sheriff Hartwell?

SHERIFF HARTWELL

I'm here. What is it?

JOE PETTIBONE

You're a hard man to find, Sheriff. I have a message here from the governor.

MAYOR

What's from the governor?

JOE PETTIBONE

It's a reprieve for Earl Williams.

SHERIFF HARTWELL

For who?

JOE PETTIBONE

Earl Williams' reprieve.

MAYOR

(to the Sheriff)

And you said there wasn't going to be a reprieve. It frightens me to think of what I'd like to do to you.

(to Pettibone)

Who else were there when he gave you this?

JOE PETTIBONE

Nobody. He was out fishing.

MAYOR

Get the governor on the phone.

JOE PETTIBONE

No, he's not there. He's out duck shooting.

MAYOR

What, already?

MAYOR

Fishing. Duck hunting. A guy who's done nothing for the last forty years but play pinochle gets elected governor, right away, thinks he's a Tarzan.

SHERIFF HARTWELL

(holding out the letter)

Read that insane, he says. Well, he knows very well Williams isn't insane.

JOE PETTIBONE

Well, I never met the man.

MAYOR

Ah, pure politics.

SHERIFF HARTWELL

It's an attempt to ruin us.

MAYOR

(reading the letter)

Dementia praecox.

SHERIFF HARTWELL

Fred, we have to think fast. What are we going to tell
the reporters?

MAYOR

The party's through in this state on account of you.

SHERIFF HARTWELL

Oh, Fred . . .

MAYOR

. . . as an afterthought, I want your resignation now.

The phone rings. Sheriff Hartwell picks it up.

SHERIFF HARTWELL

(into the phone)

Hello? Yes. Yes, this is Hartwell. What, where, where?
Holy moses. Hold the wire.

• 125 •

MAYOR

What is it?

SHERIFF HARTWELL

(to the Mayor)

They've got him, they've got Williams, they've got him.
The rifle squad has got him up at his house.

MAYOR

Hold on, hold.

SHERIFF HARTWELL

(into the phone)

Hold the wire.

MAYOR

Cover up that transfer.

SHERIFF HARTWELL

Cover up that . . .

MAYOR

No. Now listen, you never arrived with this.

JOE PETTIBONE

Yes, I did. Don't you remember?

MAYOR

Wait a minute.

JOE PETTIBONE

I came through that door, and I thought he was Sheriff Hartwell.

MAYOR

How much do you make?

JOE PETTIBONE

Huh?

MAYOR

What's your salary?

JOE PETTIBONE

$40 a week.

SHERIFF HARTWELL

(on the phone)

Now don't cut me off.

MAYOR

Would you like to make $350 a month? That's almost
a hundred dollars a week.

JOE PETTIBONE

No, I couldn't afford that. Who? Me?

MAYOR

Who do you think? Now they need a fella like you in
the city sealer's office.

JOE PETTIBONE

In the what?

MAYOR

City sealer's.

JOE PETTIBONE

You mean I should work in sealer's?

MAYOR

Yes.

SHERIFF HARTWELL

(into the phone)

No. Wait a minute. I'm in conference.

JOE PETTIBONE

No, my wife wouldn't want me to do that.

MAYOR

Why not?

JOE PETTIBONE

Well, you see my wife lives in the country with my family . . .

MAYOR

That's all right, bring them all in here. We'll pay all the expenses.

JOE PETTIBONE

No, I don't think so.

MAYOR

For heaven's sake, why not?

JOE PETTIBONE

Well, I got two kids going to school. And if they change towns, they lose a grade. They're not . . .

MAYOR

No, they won't. They'll skip a grade, and I guarantee you that they'll graduate with highest grades.

SHERIFF HARTWELL

Hold your horses, hurry up, Fred.

MAYOR

What do you say?

JOE PETTIBONE

Uh, that puts me in a kind of peculiar hole.

MAYOR

No, it doesn't. Now remember, you never delivered this.

JOE PETTIBONE

Yes, I did.

MAYOR

Oh, you didn't. You got caught in the traffic or something.

JOE PETTIBONE

No, I came around the back.

MAYOR

Well, pretend you didn't. Now get out of here, and don't let anybody see you.

JOE PETTIBONE

But how do I know that—

MAYOR

Come see me in my office tomorrow. What's your name?

JOE PETTIBONE

Pettibone. What's yours?

MAYOR

Pettibone?

JOE PETTIBONE

Not really?

MAYOR

No. No, no. All you've got to do is to lay low and keep your mouth shut.

JOE PETTIBONE

Well, I'm tired anyhow.

MAYOR

Here, go to this address. Nice homey place. They'll take good care of you. Just tell them Fred sent you. Here's $50 on account.

SHERIFF HARTWELL

(into the phone)

Will you wait, Olson? I'll tell you in one minute.

JOE PETTIBONE

Well, you forgot to tell me what the city sealer does.

MAYOR

I'll explain it all tomorrow.

JOE PETTIBONE

Is it hard?

MAYOR

No. No. Easy. Very easy.

JOE PETTIBONE

Well that's good because my health isn't what my wife . . .

MAYOR

Well, we'll fix that too.

JOE PETTIBONE

My wife?

MAYOR

Yeah. We'll fix anything. Go ahead.

SHERIFF HARTWELL

(to the Mayor)

Fred, Fred, they're still on the phone.

MAYOR

All right. Tell him to shoot to kill.

SHERIFF HARTWELL

What?

MAYOR

You heard what I said?

SHERIFF HARTWELL

But the reprieve, Fred . . .

MAYOR

All you have to do is what I tell you.

SHERIFF HARTWELL

(into the phone)

Hello, Olson. Shoot to kill. That's the orders. Pass the word around.

MAYOR

$500 reward.

SHERIFF HARTWELL

(into the phone)

$500 to the man who does it. All right, I'll be right over.

Hildy is in the newsroom. Diamond Louie comes in.

LOUIE

Hi, Hildy.

HILDY JOHNSON

You double-crossing hyena.

LOUIE

What's the matter, Hildy?

HILDY JOHNSON

Don't give me that innocent stuff. What did you pull on Mr. Baldwin this time?

LOUIE

Who? Me?

HILDY JOHNSON

Yes. You and that albino of yours.

LOUIE

You talking about Evangeline?

HILDY JOHNSON

None other.

LOUIE

She ain't an albino.

HILDY JOHNSON

She'll do until one comes along.

LOUIE

She's born right here in this country.

HILDY JOHNSON

She tries anything else, you'll have to stay right here
in . . .

LOUIE

I don't want to . . .

HILDY JOHNSON

And you too. And it won't be on a phony charge either.
Did you bring that money?

LOUIE

Oh yeah. Four hundred bucks.

HILDY JOHNSON

Four-fifty.

LOUIE

All right. You can't blame a guy for trying.

He hands over the money.

LOUIE

There. You better give me a receipt.

HILDY JOHNSON

I'll give you a scar.

LOUIE

I've got plenty of them.

HILDY JOHNSON

Oh, and I'll take Mr. Baldwin's wallet too.

LOUIE

Mr. Baldwin's what?

HILDY JOHNSON

His purse. Come on. Come on, Louie.

LOUIE

All right, Hildy.

Louie takes the wallet out of his pocket and hands it to Hildy.

DIAMOND LOUIE

I'll do it for you because I like you. But you better tell that finance of yours, he has to be more careful in these hard times. You know what I mean?

HILDY JOHNSON

Sure. Do you want him to carry brass knuckles too?

Hildy picks up her suitcase.

LOUIE

Don't talk that way, Hildy. Here, I'll take that.

He takes the suitcase from her.

LOUIE

I'll take it to the station.

HILDY JOHNSON

Wait a minute. Wait a minute. You'll take it over to the station, all right. You'll take it to the 27th Precinct and tell the cops how this all happened.

LOUIE

Can't do that, Hildy, Burns will have me in Alcatraz in an hour.

HILDY JOHNSON

That's not a bad idea. Louie!

Louie gives Hildy back her suitcase and runs off. Hildy picks up the phone.

HILDY JOHNSON

(into the phone)

Hello, operator, Hildy Johnson. Will you get me . . .

Earl Williams comes in through the window, with a pistol trained on Hildy. He looks crazed and desperate.

EARL WILLIAMS

Drop that phone.

HILDY JOHNSON

Never mind.

EARL WILLIAMS

You're not going to tell anybody where I am.

HILDY JOHNSON

Put that gun down, Earl. You don't want to shoot me, Earl, I'm your friend, remember? I'm going to write the story on your production for use.

EARL WILLIAMS

Oh yes, that's right. Production for use.

HILDY JOHNSON

You don't want to hurt your friend.

EARL WILLIAMS

No. Maybe you're my friend and maybe you're not. But don't come any nearer. You can't trust anybody in this crazy world.

The phone rings.

HILDY JOHNSON

I don't blame you, Earl. If I were you, I wouldn't trust anybody either.

She picks up the receiver.

EARL WILLIAMS

Don't do that. Put it back. Put it back. You know, if you try any tricks, I'll shoot you. I can do it right from here.

Hildy hangs up the phone.

HILDY JOHNSON

Sure you could, Earl. You don't want to do that. You don't want to kill anybody.

EARL WILLIAMS

No, you're right. I don't want to kill anybody.

HILDY JOHNSON

That's what I thought.

EARL WILLIAMS

Wait a minute, where are you going?

HILDY JOHNSON

I'm just going to close the door so nobody can see you.

EARL WILLIAMS

No, you weren't. You were going to get somebody. But I don't want that. All I want is to be left alone.

HILDY JOHNSON

I won't get nobody.

EARL WILLIAMS

Yes, you will. You'll get them after me again. I won't let you do that. I—

Hearing a noise outside the window, Earl fires. Hildy takes the gun away from him.

EARL WILLIAMS

I'm awful tired.

HILDY JOHNSON

They will hear that shot. They'll know you're here.

She rushes to close the newsroom door.

EARL WILLIAMS

I don't care. I'm not afraid to die. I was telling the fellow that when he handed me the gun—

HILDY JOHNSON

Be quiet.

EARL WILLIAMS

Waking me up in the middle of the night, talking to me about things they don't understand.

HILDY JOHNSON

Shut up.

EARL WILLIAMS

I wish they'd take me back and hang me.

Hildy hurriedly closes the windows and pulls down the shades.

HILDY JOHNSON

They will if you don't keep quiet.

EARL WILLIAMS

I couldn't go through another day like this.

HILDY JOHNSON

Well, do you I think I could?
(she picks up the phone)
Give me Walter Burns, quick. Tell him I need him.

Another phone rings. Hildy rushes to answer it.

HILDY JOHNSON

(into the phone)

Hello? Hello. Oh, but Bruce, please, I know I said I'd be down in ten minutes, but something terrific just happened. Hold on.

She rushes over to the other phone and picks it up.

HILDY JOHNSON

(into one phone)

Walter, it's Hildy; come over here right away.
(into the other phone)
Wait, Bruce, just a second and I'll explain everything.
(into this phone)
Walter, get this, I got Williams here. Here, right in the press room; it's on the level. Hurry. I need you, bye.

Hildy hangs up the first phone and speaks into the other.

HILDY JOHNSON

Bruce, best news in the world, I captured Earl Williams. You know, the murderer?

A rap on the newsroom door.

HILDY JOHNSON

Wait a minute.

(into the phone)

Listen, Bruce, I'll be down. Just as soon as I hand him over to the paper, I'll be right down. Oh, Bruce, I can't. Bruce, don't you realize? . . .

We hear a click on the phone as Bruce hangs up. A knock on the door. Hildy rushes over to it.

HILDY JOHNSON

Who is it?

MOLLIE MALLOY

(off camera)

It's me, Mollie Malloy; open the door.

Hildy opens the door for her.

HILDY JOHNSON

What do you want, Mollie?

MOLLIE MALLOY

I gotta find . . .

Mollie looks around to see an empty newsroom.

MOLLIE MALLOY

Where is everybody?

HILDY JOHNSON

They're not here. They're all gone.

MOLLIE MALLOY

Oh, please tell me where they've gone. Please tell me.

HILDY JOHNSON

Mollie, I don't know, and I'm awful busy. You wanna run along?

MOLLIE MALLOY

Oh, well, look, they got him surrounded. They're going to shoot him down like a dog.

HILDY JOHNSON

They're looking for you too. Just march on, and get out here.

MOLLIE MALLOY

I don't care. You gotta tell me, you gotta. I ain't afraid of them.

HILDY JOHNSON

All right. I'll tell you where they are there. They're on Center Street. Center and Fourth.

MOLLIE MALLOY

Oh. That's where he used to . . .

EARL WILLIAMS

Mollie. Mollie, don't go.

HILDY JOHNSON

Come in, Mollie, drop the tears.

EARL WILLIAMS

Hello, Mollie.

MOLLIE MALLOY

How did you get in here?

EARL WILLIAMS

Down the pipe. I didn't mean to shoot him. Really, I didn't.

HILDY JOHNSON

Shhh. Be quiet.

EARL WILLIAMS

You believe me, don't you, Mollie?

MOLLIE MALLOY

Sure, I believe you.

EARL WILLIAMS

Thanks for the roses. They were beautiful.

In the background, Hildy hangs up the phone.

MOLLIE MALLOY

I am going to get him out of here.

Mollie breaks down in sobs.

HILDY JOHNSON

Sit down! Are you crazy? You wouldn't get halfway down that hall without being seen.

MOLLIE MALLOY

But they will find him.

HILDY JOHNSON

I know. I know it. I'm trying to think before those reporters get back.

EARL WILLIAMS

Let them take me. What difference does it make?

MOLLIE MALLOY

No, I will not let them.

A knock on the door. We see Endicott and McCue out in the hallway.

ENDICOTT

Hey, who locked the door?

MOLLIE MALLOY

It's too late.

HILDY JOHNSON

No, it's not. Come on, get in this desk. Come here. Sit down.

She opens a rolltop desk. Williams gets into it, and she rolls the top down. She and Mollie roll a chair up in front of it. Mollie starts to sob and sits in the chair. The knocking on the door intensifies.

HILDY JOHNSON

All right. All right. I'm coming.

She opens the door and turns on the lights.

HILDY JOHNSON

What are you trying to do—kick the doors down?

Endicott and McCue come in.

ENDICOTT

You're getting that exclusive, ain't you? We got some phone calls to make.

MCCUE

(seeing Mollie)

Hey, what's she doing up there?

HILDY JOHNSON

Run down and get some smelling salts, will you?

ENDICOTT

Hey, what's the matter?

MCCUE

What happened?

HILDY JOHNSON

Came up here and had hysterics. Pretty sick.

ENDICOTT

How do you feel, kid?

MOLLIE MALLOY

I don't feel so good.

MCCUE

You want some water?

HILDY JOHNSON

I'll get it.

ENDICOTT

Do you want anything for it?

MOLLIE MALLOY

No.

MCCUE

No, you don't so look sick to me.

ENDICOTT

Hey, you didn't bump into Williams, did you?

MOLLIE MALLOY

Ain't you funny?

MCCUE

Hey, where is he?

MOLLIE MALLOY

Lemme alone, will you?

MCCUE

(into the phone)

Okay. Give me the desk.

(to Mollie)

No harm in asking.

(into the phone)

Hello, Jim, it's a false alarm. They surrounded the house, all right. But they forgot to tell Williams, and he wasn't there.

Murphy comes in, followed by Wilson and Bensinger. Murphy goes to his phone.

MURPHY

(into the phone)

Halloween going on outside, the whole police force standing on its ear.

(to Hildy)

Hello, Hildy, we thought you were gone.

HILDY JOHNSON

Waiting for some money from Walter.

MCCUE

(into the phone)

What a chase. Give me Emo.

HILDY JOHNSON

Any news, boys?

WILSON

Yeah, I've never been so tired in my life.

MCCUE

(into the phone)

What way? Melrose Station? Huh? All right, connect me.

Hello, Mollie, how are you? Hold it a minute. Hey, fellas. This looks good.

MURPHY

(into the phone)

Yeah. Call you back.

MCCUE

Old lady just called the detective bureau, claims Williams is hiding under her piazza.

MURPHY

Tell her to stand up.

ENDICOTT

We looked every other place.

MCCUE

Did you want to go out on it?

HILDY JOHNSON

I have to stick around. I'll cover this end for you.

MURPHY

I've spent $1.40 on taxi cabs already.

ENDICOTT

Let's not do any more going out.

MCCUE

(into the phone)

Never mind, sir. Just tear it up.

MURPHY

Hey, who pulled the shades down?

HILDY JOHNSON

I did. They were throwing those lights around.

Murphy pulls open a shade and looks out the window.

MURPHY

(looking out the window)

You know, I got a hunch Williams isn't anywhere they've been looking for him.

McCue walks up behind Murphy.

MCCUE

He might be right here in this building somewhere.

HILDY JOHNSON

Sure, sure. Hanging around like a duck in a shooting gallery.

Wilson goes over to the windows and opens another shade.

WILSON

It was that skylight he got out of, but how did he reach the ground?

MCCUE

I'm pretending it rained in here all night.

MURPHY

Jump over to this roof.

ENDICOTT

It's only about twelve feet.

WILSON

Yeah, once he got to the roof, he could slide down a drain pipe.

MCCUE

And come in any one of these windows on this side.

ENDICOTT

The story's going to walk right in the window.

HILDY JOHNSON

Master minds at work. Why don't you boys go home? Maybe Williams will come and call on you.

MURPHY

Wouldn't it be funny if he's in this building some-where?

HILDY JOHNSON

Well, why not search the building? Everybody take a floor.

MURPHY

No, I'm not going to wander all over this place.

HILDY JOHNSON

A great bunch of reporters you are. The biggest story in two years, and you're all too lazy to go out.

MURPHY

Say Hildy, if I know you, you seem pretty anxious to get rid of us. You trying to scoop us or something?

MCCUE

What is that?

HILDY JOHNSON

What, are you crazy? On my own time?

WILSON

She's been giving the story on how Williams got the gun.

MALE SPEAKER

Hey, did you smuggle that gun in to Williams, Mollie?

MOLLIE MALLOY

Oh, no. I didn't do nothing.

WILSON

Come clean, Mollie.

HILDY JOHNSON

Will you let the girl alone? She said . . .

Bruce's mother, Mrs. Baldwin, a very stiff and upright old woman, comes in. She is in a very righteous mood.

MRS. BALDWIN

Well.

HILDY JOHNSON

Mrs. Baldwin! Mother!

MRS. BRUCE BALDWIN

Don't you "mother" me, playing cat and mouse with my poor boy, keeping him locked up, making him miss two trains.

HILDY JOHNSON

I can explain.

MRS. BRUCE BALDWIN

And you supposed to be married tomorrow.

HILDY JOHNSON

I will be with you in five minutes.

MRS. BRUCE BALDWIN

You don't have to go with me at all. Just give me Bruce's money and you can stay here forever as far as I'm concerned. You and that murderer you caught.

MCCUE

What's that?

MRS. BRUCE BALDWIN

Which one of these men is it? They all look like murderers to me.

MURPHY

Wait a minute, Hildy, what murderer did you catch?

HILDY JOHNSON

I wasn't talking about that. I haven't said any such thing.

Mollie is watching them, looking back and forth at the desk where Murphy is hiding. She looks more and more distressed.

MRS. BRUCE BALDWIN

I'm quoting my son, and he has never lied to me.

MCCUE

Come on.

HILDY JOHNSON

Don't be ridiculous. In the first place, I never said anything like that.

MRS. BRUCE BALDWIN

Yes, you did.

HILDY JOHNSON

No, I didn't. I said I was uh, trying to find the murderer. She got it all balled up. Can't you see that?

MURPHY

Who are you holding?

HILDY JOHNSON

Nobody.

MCCUE

Come clean.

HILDY JOHNSON

Let me go, will you? I don't know where he is.

MOLLIE MALLOY

Stop! Stop!! What are you asking her for? She don't
know where he is. I'm the only one that knows.

MURPHY

Where is Williams?

MOLLIE MALLOY

Try and find out.

MCCUE

Come on, Mollie, talk.

MOLLIE MALLOY

Talk. Now you want me to talk.

MURPHY

Sure.

MOLLIE MALLOY

Oh, isn't that funny? You wouldn't listen to me before.
Not even for a minute. Now you want me to talk?

HILDY JOHNSON

Don't tell anything, Mollie.

MOLLIE MALLOY

Leave me alone. I know what I'm doing.

MCCUE

Stay out of this, Hildy.

MOLLIE MALLOY

Why didn't you listen to me? Why?

MURPHY

Come on. Cut that out.

MOLLIE MALLOY

You keep your hands off me.

MURPHY

Where is he?

MOLLIE MALLOY

What do you want to know for? So you can write some more lies, so you can sell some more papers?

MCCUE

Never mind that.

MOLLIE MALLOY

All right. All right. I'll tell you what I'll do. I'll give you a story. I'll give you a wonderful story. Only this time it'll be true. You'll never find him now.

Mollie Malloy rushes to the window and jumps out. The reporters rush to the window and look down. Several policemen are surrounding the fallen Mollie. Walter and Diamond Louie walk into the press room.

MURPHY

Get the ambulance, somebody. Get the ambulance, somebody.

She's dead.

MURPHY

No, she isn't, see, she's moving.

The reporters rush out of the press room. Walter comes over to the window.

HILDY JOHNSON

Walter, did you see that?

WALTER BURNS

Where is he?

HILDY JOHNSON

She jumped out the window.

WALTER BURNS

I know that. Where is he, I said?

HILDY JOHNSON

She isn't dead.

WALTER BURNS

Hildy, where have you got Williams?

HILDY JOHNSON

He's in the desk. I hope she didn't kill herself.

Walter goes to the desk and opens it a little.

WALTER BURNS

How are you doing, Earl?

EARL WILLIAMS

Let me out. I can't stand it.

WALTER BURNS

Keep quiet, you're sitting pretty.

MRS. BALDWIN

What's in there?

WALTER BURNS

Who are you?

MRS. BALDWIN

What are you doing?

WALTER BURNS

Who is she?

HILDY JOHNSON

This is Mrs. Baldwin, Bruce's mother.

MRS. BALDWIN

What are you doing?

WALTER BURNS

Shut up.

MRS. BALDWIN

I won't shut up. You are doing something wrong.

HILDY JOHNSON

Mother, please.

WALTER BURNS

Take her out of here.

HILDY JOHNSON

Wait a minute, Walter.

WALTER BURNS

Don't worry. Louie.

LOUIE

Yes, boss.

WALTER BURNS

Take the lady over to Polack Mike's.

LOUIE

(to Mrs. Baldwin)

My name's Louis Paluzzo.

Louie hoists Mrs. Baldwin over his shoulder and carries her out.

WALTER BURNS

Lock her up. See she doesn't talk to anyone on your way.

HILDY JOHNSON

Walter, you can't do this.

LOUIE

What should I tell him?

WALTER BURNS

Tell him it's a case of DTs.

HILDY JOHNSON

Don't worry, mother. This is only temporary.

Louie hauls Mrs. Baldwin out of the newsroom. Walter closes the door behind them. Hildy makes to go out, but Walter grabs her by the forearms.

HILDY JOHNSON

Walter, let go of me.

WALTER BURNS

Where do you think you're going?

HILDY JOHNSON

I'm going after mother. I'm going to get Bruce out of jail. Walter, why did you have to do this to me?

WALTER BURNS

Get Bruce out of jail? How can you worry about a man who's resting in a nice quiet police station while this is going on? Hildy, this is war. You can't desert me now.

HILDY JOHNSON

Oh, Walter, would you get off that trapeze? You've got your story right over there on the desk. Go on. Smear it all over the front page. Earl Williams captured by the Morning Post. I covered your story for you and I got into a fine mess doing it. Now I'm getting out.

WALTER BURNS

You drooling idiot. What do you mean, you're getting out?

HILDY JOHNSON

Just what I said.

WALTER BURNS

There are 365 days in a year, one can get mad. How many times you got a murderer locked up in a desk? Once in a lifetime, Hildy, you got the whole city by the seat of the pants.

HILDY JOHNSON

Yeah, I know, I know.

WALTER BURNS

You know, you know you've got the brain of a pancake. This isn't just a story you're covering. It's a revolution. This is the greatest yarn in journalism since Livingston discovered Stanley.

HILDY JOHNSON

It's the other way around.

WALTER BURNS

Oh, don't get technical at a time like this. You realize what you've done, honey. You've taken a city that's been graft-ridden for forty years under the same old gang; with this yarn, you're kicking them out. You're giving us a chance to have the same kind of government New York's having under La Guardia. Listen, honey, if I didn't have your best interests at heart, you think I'd waste my time arguing with you? You've done something big, Hildy. You stepped up into a new class.

HILDY JOHNSON

Huh?

WALTER BURNS

We'll make such monkeys out of those ward heelers next Tuesday, nobody will vote for them, not even their wives.

HILDY JOHNSON

Expose them, eh?

WALTER BURNS

Certainly. We'll crucify that mob. We keep Williams undercover until morning. So the Post can break the story exclusive. Then we let the governor in on the capture, share the glory with him.

HILDY JOHNSON

I get it, I get it.

WALTER BURNS

You kick over the whole city hall like an upper cut. You got the Mayor all backed up against the wall. You put one administration out and another one in. This isn't just a newspaper story, Hildy. It's a career. And you stand there bellyaching about whether you catch an eight o'clock train or a nine o'clock train.

HILDY JOHNSON

Well, I never figured it that way.

WALTER BURNS

You're still a doll-faced hick, that's why.

HILDY JOHNSON

You'd be the white-haired boy.

WALTER BURNS

Sure. They'll be naming streets after you, Hildy John-son Street. There'll be statues of you in the park. The movies will be after you, the radio. By tomorrow morn-ing, I bet you there'll be a Hildy Johnson cigar, and I can see the billboard now that says, "Light up with Hildy Johnson!"

HILDY JOHNSON

Oh, Walter, will you stop that acting?

WALTER BURNS

Huh?

HILDY JOHNSON

We got a lot to do.

WALTER BURNS

Now you're talking.

HILDY JOHNSON

We can't leave Williams in here.

WALTER BURNS

We'll take him over to my private office. Which is our phone?

HILDY JOHNSON

That one over. How are you going to take him? They'll see him.

Walter goes over to the phone.

WALTER BURNS

Not if he's inside the desk. We carry the desk over. Hello?

HILDY JOHNSON

You can't move that desk. It's crawling with cops outside.

WALTER BURNS

All right, we'll lower it out the window with pulleys. Now quit stalling. Get the typewriter over here and start pounding out a lede!

Hildy brings the typewriter over to the main table and starts typing.

HILDY JOHNSON

How much of the stuff do you want?

WALTER BURNS

All the words you got.

Walter picks up the phone and speaks into it.

WALTER BURNS

Hello! Give me Duffy.

HILDY JOHNSON

Walter?

WALTER BURNS

What?

HILDY JOHNSON

Can I call the Mayor a bird of prey?

WALTER BURNS

Call him anything you like.

HILDY JOHNSON

How about the time he had his house painted by the fire department?

WALTER BURNS

Give him the works. Hello, Duffy. Get set. We got the biggest story in years. Earl Williams captured by the Morning Post. Exclusive. Yeah, but I want you to tear up the whole front page. That's what I said, the whole front page out. Never mind the European war, we got something a whole lot bigger than that. Hildy Johnson's writing the lede, I'll give it to you soon she's finished. And listen, Duffy, get hold of Butch O'Connor, tell him to come up here right away with half a dozen of his wrestlers. Yeah, Butch O'Connor. What? Well, I got a desk I want to move.

Bruce Baldwin comes in and takes off his hat.

BRUCE BALDWIN

Hildy.

WALTER BURNS

What the deuce do you want?

HILDY JOHNSON

Hello, Bruce.

WALTER BURNS

(into the phone)

No, no, never mind that Chinese earthquake, for heaven's sake.

BRUCE BALDWIN

Hildy, I just want to ask you one question.

HILDY JOHNSON

Bruce, how did you get out of jail?

BRUCE BALDWIN

Well, not through any help of yours . . .

WALTER BURNS

Now listen, buddy, you can't come in here.

BRUCE BALDWIN

I am not talking to you. I had to wire Albany for a hundred dollars so I could get out on bail.

WALTER BURNS

(into the phone)

No, I don't care if there's a million there.

BRUCE BALDWIN

I don't know what they're going to think up there in Albany. They had to send the money to the police station.

WALTER BURNS

Oh, for Pete's sake, Hildy, come on, we're waiting for that story.

HILDY JOHNSON

I'll explain everything to them, Bruce.

BRUCE BALDWIN

Well, where's Mother? She said she was coming up here

HILDY JOHNSON

Oh, she left.

WALTER BURNS

(into the phone)

No, I can't hear you, Duffy.

BRUCE BALDWIN

Where did she go?

Hildy is typing rapidly.

HILDY JOHNSON

Out someplace.

WALTER BURNS

(into the phone)

No. Dump the Polish corridor.

BRUCE BALDWIN

Hildy, tell me where my mother was going.

HILDY JOHNSON

She couldn't say.

WALTER BURNS

(into the phone)

Oh, never mind that, this is more important.

BRUCE BALDWIN

Did she get the money from you?

HILDY JOHNSON

Oh no. No. She left in a hurry.

WALTER BURNS

I'll take that money, Hildy.

HILDY JOHNSON

All right, Bruce, it's right there in my purse.

BRUCE BALDWIN

I've decided I can handle the things around here, and I'll take that certified check too.

HILDY JOHNSON

I'll give it to you, Bruce, here. Here, you can take it. So you'll find your money in your wallet.

Hildy hands Bruce his wallet. He pulls out the $450.

BRUCE BALDWIN

My wallet. This is my wallet. Say, there's something funny going on.

Walter takes the money and examines it.

BRUCE BALDWIN

Hey, what are you doing?

WALTER BURNS

Just wanted to look at it.

BRUCE BALDWIN

Hildy, I am taking . . .

WALTER BURNS

Uh, Duff, what did say?

BRUCE BALDWIN

Hildy, I'm taking the nine o'clock train.

HILDY JOHNSON

Good, good.

But she keeps on typing.

BRUCE BALDWIN

Did you hear what I said? I said I'm taking the nine o'clock.

HILDY JOHNSON

Nine o'clock.

She rips the page out of the typewriter.

HILDY JOHNSON

Oh, Bruce, I put it in here.

WALTER BURNS

Hey, let her alone, will you, buddy?

HILDY JOHNSON

Will you do me a favor, Bruce, please?

Hildy puts a new sheet of paper in the typewriter.

BRUCE BALDWIN

Hildy, I just want you to answer one question, if you
don't want to come with me . . .

Hildy snatches another piece of paper.

HILDY JOHNSON

I need that.

BRUCE BALDWIN

Answer me.

WALTER BURNS

Come on.

BRUCE BALDWIN

You don't, do you?

WALTER BURNS

(into the phone)

No. Take all those Miss America pictures off page six.

BRUCE BALDWIN

Hildy, tell me. Please tell me the truth.

WALTER BURNS

(into the phone)

Oh, wait a minute.

BRUCE BALDWIN

Did you ever love me, Hildy?

WALTER BURNS

(to Bruce)

Now look here, my good man . . .

BRUCE BALDWIN

You shut up, Burns.

HILDY JOHNSON

Well, how can I do anything with . . .

BRUCE BALDWIN

You're doing all this to her. I know that. She wanted to get away from you and everything you stand for, but you were too smart. You caught her and changed her mind.

WALTER BURNS

(into the phone)

Take Hitler and stick him on the funny page.

(to Bruce Baldwin)

Now, let me ask you, Mr. whatever your name is . . .

BRUCE BALDWIN

You're doing all this for a man like him?

HILDY JOHNSON

No, I am not, but Bruce, can't you see that something has happened? Wait, I'll tell you everything.

WALTER BURNS

Tell him? You'll tell him nothing. He's a spy, you fool.

HILDY JOHNSON

Don't be ridiculous.

BRUCE BALDWIN

I'm not a spy. Come on, Hildy, you're coming with me right now.

HILDY JOHNSON

Give me just a second, can't you, don't you see this is the biggest thing in my life?

WALTER BURNS

Keep quiet, Hildy.

BRUCE BALDWIN

I see. I'll keep. I'm like something in the icebox, aren't I?

WALTER BURNS

Yeah.

BRUCE BALDWIN

You just don't love me.

HILDY JOHNSON

Oh, now, that isn't true. Just because I won't listen, you say I don't love you. Now you know that isn't the point at all.

WALTER BURNS

(into the phone)

What else . . .

BRUCE BALDWIN

The point is you never intended to be decent and live like a human being.

WALTER BURNS

What's that?

HILDY JOHNSON

All right. All right. You can think what you want to think.

WALTER BURNS

All right. Stop bursting and jumping, I'm trying to concentrate.

BRUCE BALDWIN

You're just like him and all the rest.

HILDY JOHNSON

Oh, sure, that's what I am.

WALTER BURNS

(into the phone)

What? What? No, no. Leave the rooster story alone. That's human interest. Did you get hold of Butch O'Connor yet?

HILDY JOHNSON

You don't understand.

BRUCE BALDWIN

I understand, all right, I understand.

HILDY JOHNSON

Wait, wait just a minute. There's only one question I want to know.

BRUCE BALDWIN

What?

HILDY JOHNSON

Walter, the Mayor's first wife, what was her name?

WALTER BURNS

(to Hildy)

You mean the one with the wart? Fanny.

(into the phone)

What did you say, Duffy?

BRUCE BALDWIN

All right, Hildy, I don't think you ever loved me at all.

WALTER BURNS

(into the phone)

Oh, never mind that, you're not working for the advertising department.

BRUCE BALDWIN

Remember, if you change your mind, I'm leaving on the nine o'clock train.

Bruce goes out, but Hildy doesn't notice; throughout all this she has been typing. Walter runs over and locks the door.

HILDY JOHNSON

Bruce, you've got to take me as I am instead of trying to change me into something else. I'm no suburban bridge player. I'm a newspaper man.

WALTER BURNS

Don't stop, Hildy. Keep it coming. Go as fast as you can.

Earl Williams rolls up the desk front.

WALTER BURNS

(to Williams)

Get back in there, you mock turtle.

(into the phone)

Hello, Duffy, did you tell Butch and his gang to take a taxi, this is a matter of life and death? Good. Stay on this wire. Butch is on his way over. All we got to do is hold out for fifteen minutes.

HILDY JOHNSON

The boys will be back coming in here to phone.

WALTER BURNS

I'll handle them.

Walter goes to the window and looks out.

WALTER BURNS

Oh no, now, the moon's out!

Walter raps three times on the desk. Earl Williams raps back.

• 173 •

WALTER BURNS

Fine. Three taps is me, don't forget. How you doing?
Got enough air?

EARL WILLIAMS

Not very much.

Walter opens the desk, waves some air a couple of times
toward it, and closes it again.

WALTER BURNS

That better? You're sitting pretty. How's it coming,
hun?

HILDY JOHNSON

Oh, all right, I guess . . . Where's Bruce?

WALTER BURNS

Bruce. Oh, he went out.

HILDY JOHNSON

Is he coming back here?

WALTER BURNS

He said he's coming back. Didn't you hear him? What
have you got so far? Let me hear.

HILDY JOHNSON

"While hundreds of Sheriff Hartwell's paid gunmen
stalk the city, shooting innocent bystanders, spread-
ing their reign of terror, Earl Williams was lurking
less than twenty hours . . ."

WALTER BURNS

Wait a minute. Wait a minute. Aren't you going to mention the Post? Doesn't the paper get any credit?

HILDY JOHNSON

Well, I did that right there in the second paragraph.

WALTER BURNS

Who's going to read the second paragraph? Listen, honey, for ten years I've been telling you how to write a newspaper story, and that's what I get?

HILDY JOHNSON

Oh, I'm sorry.

Outside the room, Bensinger knocks on the door.

BENSINGER

What's the idea of locking this door?

WALTER BURNS

Who's that?

HILDY JOHNSON

Bensinger. That's his desk.

Hildy points toward the one Williams is hiding in.

BENSINGER

Open the door, will you?

WALTER BURNS

Hildy, what did you say his name was?

HILDY JOHNSON

Bensinger, he works for the Tribune.

WALTER BURNS

Tribune, huh?

BENSINGER

Who's in there? You have any better sense than to . . .

They let Bensinger in. He sees Walter.

BENSINGER

Uh, hello. Hello, Mr. Burns. Well, quite an honor having you come over here.

WALTER BURNS

Hello, Bensinger.

BENSINGER

Oh, you know my . . . Excuse me. I just want to get my . . .

WALTER BURNS

Oh, you know, it's quite a coincidence seeing you tonight, isn't it, Hildy?

HILDY JOHNSON

Yes. Yes.

BENSINGER

How do you mean?

WALTER BURNS

As a matter of fact, I was talking to our Mr. Duffy about you just this afternoon.

BENSINGER

Really? Well, nothing detrimental, I hope.

WALTER BURNS

On the contrary. On the contrary, that was one swell story you had in the paper this morning.

BENSINGER

Oh, did you, uh, did you care for the poem, Mr. Burns?

WALTER BURNS

Uh, the poem? The poem was great.

BENSINGER

I like the ending, especially "and all is well outside his cell. But in his heart, he hears the hangman calling and the gallows falling and his white-haired mother's tears." Heartbreaking.

WALTER BURNS

That's fine. How'd you like to come and work for me?

BENSINGER

What?

WALTER BURNS

Yes, we can use a man like you. All we have now is a lot of lowbrows, like Johnson here.

BENSINGER

Are you serious, Mr. Burns?

WALTER BURNS

Serious? Wait a minute.

Walter goes over to the phone.

WALTER

(into the phone)

Duffy, Duffy, I'm sending you Mr. Benginer over to see
you.

BENSINGER

No, Bensinger.

WALTER BURNS

Oh yeah. And Mervin, isn't it?

BENSINGER

Yeah. No. Roy. Roy V.

WALTER BURNS

(into the phone)

Certainly, Roy V. Bensinger, the poet. Well, of course
you wouldn't know. You've probably never heard of
Shakespeare either. Now look, I want you to put Mr.
Bensinger on the staff right away. How much are you
getting on the Tribune, Roy?

BENSINGER

Ah, 75.

WALTER BURNS

I'll give you a hundred and a byline. Now you give him everything he wants. You understand? Okay. Now look, Roy, I want you to hustle and write me a story from the point of view of the escaped man. He hides cowering, afraid of every sound, of every light. He hears footsteps. His heart is going like that. And all the time they're closing in. Now get the sense of the animal at bay.

BENSINGER

Sort of a Jack London style?

WALTER BURNS

Exactly.

BENSINGER

I'll just get my rhyming dictionary.

Bensinger goes toward his desk.

WALTER BURNS

Doesn't have to rhyme. Doesn't have to rhyme.

BENSINGER

Oh, well I'm deeply grateful, Mr. Burns. It's very—oh, if you should have an opening for a war correspondent, I parlay a little French. You know?

WALTER BURNS

I'll keep you in mind.

BENSINGER

Au revoir, mon capitaine.

WALTER BURNS

Bonjour.

**The two men give each other mock salutes. Bensinger leaves
and Walter closes the door.**

WALTER BURNS

"His white-haired mother's tears" that's a laugh.

(into the phone)

Now listen, that Bensinger is on his way over to see
you right now. Handle him with kid gloves. Put him to
work writing poetry. No, no. We don't want him. Just
stall him along until the extra's out, then tell him his
poetry smells and kick him downstairs.

HILDY JOHNSON

Double-crossing swine.

WALTER BURNS

You said it. That'll teach him a lesson. He won't quit
his paper without giving notice after this.

HILDY JOHNSON

I mean you.

WALTER BURNS

Me?

HILDY JOHNSON

You'll double-cross anybody . . . Wait a minute.

WALTER BURNS

What?

HILDY JOHNSON

I just remembered. Bruce isn't coming back here. He said he was taking the nine o'clock train.

WALTER BURNS

Oh, well in that case, he's gone by now. Come on, honey, don't sit there like a frozen robin. Get on with the story. You ought to have our ledes all finished by the time Butch gets here.

HILDY JOHNSON

How you have messed up my life! What am I going to do?

Walter measures the window and then the desk by hand.

WALTER BURNS

The window's too small. We have to carry the desk out of the building.

HILDY JOHNSON

He might be on the train right now.

WALTER BURNS

Come on. Come on.

HILDY JOHNSON

What a fool I was, falling for you. "Oh, they're going to name streets after you. Johnson Street."

WALTER BURNS

Yes. Well, you've had a nice rest. Now get back to work.

HILDY JOHNSON

I'm not going back to work. Walter!

A knock on the door.

WALTER BURNS

Who is it?

LOUIE

(off camera)

It's me, boss. It's Louie.

Walter lets Louie in. He looks very disheveled.

WALTER BURNS

Louie! Holy smoke, what's the matter with you?

HILDY JOHNSON

Where is Mrs. Baldwin?

WALTER BURNS

What did you do with her?

HILDY JOHNSON

What happened?

WALTER BURNS

Have you been in a fight?

LOUIE

Down West Avenue, we was going sixty-five miles an hour. You know what I mean?

WALTER BURNS

Take that mush out of your mouth.

HILDY JOHNSON

Where is the old lady?

LOUIE

I am telling you. We went smack into a police patrol. You know what I mean? We busted it in half.

HILDY JOHNSON

What she hurt?

WALTER BURNS

Look, where is she? Tell me.

LOUIE

Imagine bumping into a load of cops to come rolling out like oranges.

HILDY JOHNSON

What did you do with her?

LOUIE

Oh, search me! When I come too, I was running down Thirty-fifth Street.

HILDY JOHNSON

You were with her, weren't you?

LOUIE

Was I?

HILDY JOHNSON

You were in the taxicab.

LOUIE

The driver got knocked cold.

WALTER BURNS

Butterfingers! I give you an old lady to take care of, and you hand her over to the cops.

LOUIE

What do you mean I handed her? The cops was on the wrong side of the street.

WALTER BURNS

Now everything's fine. She's probably squawking her head off in the police station.

LOUIE

I don't think she's squawking much. You know what I mean?

HILDY JOHNSON

Don't tell me. Was she killed?

WALTER BURNS

Hey, was she? Did you notice?

LOUIE

See, listen, me with a gun on the hip and a kidnapped old lady on my hands, I'm going to stick around asking questions from a lot of cops? You know what I mean?

HILDY JOHNSON

Dead. Dead. Oh, this is the end, oh.

WALTER BURNS

It's fate, Hildy. What will be, will be.

HILDY JOHNSON

What am I going to say to Bruce? What can I tell him?

WALTER BURNS

Look, honey, if he really loves you, you won't have to tell him anything. Snap out of it. Would you rather have had the old dame dragging the whole police force in here?

HILDY JOHNSON

I killed her. I'm responsible. What am I going to do? How can I ever face Bruce again?

WALTER BURNS

Look at me, Hildy.

HILDY JOHNSON

I am looking at you, you murderer.

WALTER BURNS

Oh, now, if it was my own grandmother, I'd carry on. You know I would, for the paper.

HILDY JOHNSON

Louie, where did it happen?

LOUIE

Western and Thirty-fourth.

HILDY JOHNSON

I've gotta . . .

She is about to get up and go off.

WALTER BURNS

We can do more here. Now be calm.

A phone rings. Walter answers it.

WALTER

(into the phone)

Hello! Hello!!

Hildy picks up another phone.

HILDY JOHNSON

(into a phone)

Main, 4457.

WALTER BURNS

(into a phone)

Who? Well, Butch, where are you?

They cross-talk on their respective phones.

HILDY JOHNSON

(into the phone)

Oh, Mission Hospital, receiving room, please.

WALTER BURNS

(into the phone)

Oh, what are you doing there? Haven't you even started?

HILDY JOHNSON

(into the phone)

Hello, Eddie, It's Hildy Johnson. Was an old lady brought in there from an auto smash-up?

WALTER BURNS

(into the phone)

Oh for H. Sebastian, Butch! Listen, it's a matter of life and death.

HILDY JOHNSON

(into the phone)

Nobody?

WALTER BURNS

(into the phone)

I can't hear.

HILDY JOHNSON

(into the phone)

Morningside 469.

WALTER BURNS

(into the phone)

Speak up. Now what? But you can't stop for a dame now.

HILDY JOHNSON

(into the phone)

The community hospital. Give me the receiving room.

WALTER BURNS

(into the phone)

I don't care if you've been after her for six years, Butch, your whole life's at stake. You're going to let a woman come between us, after all we've been through?

HILDY JOHNSON

(into the phone)

Max, it's Hildy Johnson, was an old lady brought in there, all smashed up?

WALTER BURNS

(into the phone)

Butch, I'd put my arm in the fire for you, up to here. Now you can't double-cross me.

HILDY JOHNSON

(into the phone)

Well, look around, will you, please?

WALTER BURNS

(into the phone)

All right, put her on. I'll talk to her. Oh, good evening, Madam. Now listen, you ten-cent glamour girl, you can't keep Butch away from his duty. What's that? You say that again, I'll come over there and kick you in the teeth. Hey, what kind of language is that? Now look here, you . . . She's hung up. What did I say?

Walter picks up another phone and talks into it.

WALTER BURNS

(into the phone)

Duffy, how would you like that. Do something. Duffy!

HILDY JOHNSON

(to Walter)

You shut up, I'm trying to hear.

WALTER BURNS

(into the phone)

Duffy? That's cooperation. Duffy? Well, where is Duffy? Diabetes! I ought to know better than to hire anybody with a disease.

HILDY JOHNSON

Now give me Olympia 211.

Louie comes back in, probably from the men's room, where he has been washing up.

WALTER BURNS

Louie!

LOUIE

Yes, boss?

WALTER BURNS

Louie, it's up to you.

LOUIE

Anything you say, boss.

WALTER BURNS

Beat it out. Get hold of some guys.

LOUIE

Who do you want?

WALTER BURNS

Anybody with hair on his chest. Get them off the street. Get them anywhere. Offer them anything. Only get them. We got to get that desk out of here.

LOUIE

Is it important?

WALTER BURNS

Is it important? Louie, listen, you're the best friend I got.

LOUIE

I like you too, boss.

WALTER BURNS

All right then. Don't fail me. Get enough people to move that desk. Now come on, I'm relying on you.

LOUIE

You know me, boss, the shirt off my back.

WALTER BURNS

Okay. Don't bump into anything.

Louie goes out. Walter locks the door behind him.

That dumb immigrant will flop on me as sure as you're born.

HILDY JOHNSON

(into the phone)

We'll try again at the hospital.

WALTER BURNS

Well, if he's not back in five minutes, we carry it out alone.

HILDY JOHNSON

(to Walter)

Do anything you want.

WALTER BURNS

There's a million ways. We can start a fire, have the firemen take it out in the confusion.

HILDY JOHNSON

I don't give a darn what you do.

WALTER BURNS

Hey! Come here. See if we can lift it.

HILDY JOHNSON

(into the phone)

Oh, nobody. Oh, never mind.

Hildy hangs up the phone. Walter goes over to the desk and tries to pick up one end of it.

WALTER BURNS

Are you going to help me?

HILDY JOHNSON

No, I'm not.

WALTER BURNS

Do you want me to strain my back?

HILDY JOHNSON

I'm going to find Mrs. Baldwin.

She opens the door.

WALTER BURNS

Don't open that door.

HILDY JOHNSON

I'm going to find . . .

The reporters, along with Sheriff Hartwell, storm into the room. They grab Hildy and push her back.

HILDY

Hey, let go. What's the idea? Get your hands off me.

SHERIFF HARTWELL

Now look here, Johnson.

WALTER BURNS

Hey, you.

SHERIFF HARTWELL

You mean me?

WALTER BURNS

Yes, you. What do you mean by breaking in here like this?

SHERIFF HARTWELL

You can't bluff me, Burns. I don't care who you are or what paper you work for.

HILDY JOHNSON

Look, let go of me.

SHERIFF HARTWELL

Hang on to her.

HILDY JOHNSON

Oh please, look, fellows, something has happened to my mother-in-law.

MCCUE

We know what you are up to, Hildy.

ENDICOTT

She might be going out to get Williams.

MURPHY

She had the door locked.

WILSON

And while they're in here talking . . .

MCCUE

They know where he is.

HILDY JOHNSON

Oh look, I don't know anything, really, and there's been an accident.

SHERIFF HARTWELL

Johnson, there's something very, very peculiar going on here. Now see here, Johnson . . .

WALTER BURNS

Just a moment, Hartwell, if you have any accusations to make, make them in the proper manner. Otherwise, I'll have to ask you to get out.

SHERIFF HARTWELL

You'll ask me to what?

WALTER BURNS

Get out.

SHERIFF HARTWELL

Oh, you will, eh?

(to the policeman)

Hey, you keep that door close and don't let anybody in or out. Now we'll see about this.

MURPHY

Come on, Pinky, give 'em in the third degree.

ENDICOTT

Make 'em talk and you got Williams, Pinky.

SHERIFF HARTWELL

Yes. Now look here, Johnson, I'm going to get to the bottom of this. Are you going to talk or aren't you?

HILDY JOHNSON

Well, what do you want me to say?

SHERIFF HARTWELL

What do you know about William?

HILDY JOHNSON

What do you know about Williams?

SHERIFF HARTWELL

Now we're getting somewhere . . . All right boys, take her out of here.

HILDY JOHNSON

Oh, no, you don't. Don't you dare touch me.

They grab hold of her and a gun falls out of her purse.

ENDICOTT

Oh, crap. She's got a gun. Grab it.

HILDY JOHNSON

Oh, no you don't. Walter?

SHERIFF HARTWELL

All right, Burns, I'll take that gun. Where did you get this gun?

HILDY JOHNSON

I've got a right to carry a gun if I want to.

SHERIFF HARTWELL

Not this gun.

WALTER BURNS

I can explain that, Hartwell. When Hildy told me she was going to interview Earl Williams, I thought it would be dangerous. So I gave her a gun to defend herself.

SHERIFF HARTWELL

Oh, you did? Well that's very interesting. But this happens to be the gun that Williams used to shoot his way out with.

WALTER BURNS

All right, good man, are trying to make me out a liar?

SHERIFF HARTWELL

I ought to know my own gun.

WILSON

Oh, so that's where Williams got the gun.

SHERIFF HARTWELL

Hildy got it from Williams. Where is Earl Williams? Where have you got him?

WALTER BURNS

You're barking up the wrong tree, Hartwell.

SHERIFF HARTWELL

I'll give you three minutes to tell me where he is.

HILDY JOHNSON

He went over to the hospital to call on Professor Eggel-hoffer.

SHERIFF HARTWELL

What?

HILDY JOHNSON

With a bag of marshmallows.

MURPHY

Where is he? Ask the master mind what he's doing here.

SHERIFF HARTWELL

(to Walter)

Speak up. Speak up. What do you know about this?

WALTER BURNS

My dear fellow.

MURPHY

What is it?

WALTER BURNS

The Morning Post does not obstruct justice or hide criminals.

HILDY JOHNSON

You ought to know that.

SHERIFF HARTWELL

Johnson, you are under arrest.

HILDY JOHNSON

What?

SHERIFF HARTWELL

And you too, Burns.

WALTER BURNS

Who is under arrest? Listen, you insignificant square-toed pimple-headed spy. Do you realize what you're doing?

SHERIFF HARTWELL

I'll show you what I'm doing. Burns, you're obstructing justice, and so is the Morning Post, and I'm going to see that you're fined $10,000.

WALTER BURNS

You'll see nothing of the kind.

SHERIFF HARTWELL

And I'm going to begin by impounding the Post property. Is this your desk?

HILDY JOHNSON

No.

WALTER BURNS

Yes. What are you afraid of, Hildy?

(to the Sheriff)

I dare you to move this desk out of here.

SHERIFF HARTWELL

Oh, you do?

Yes. Go ahead and try it.

SHERIFF HARTWELL

All right, I will.

WALTER BURNS

I warn you, you move this desk out of this building and I'll put you behind bars.

HILDY JOHNSON

He can do it too.

SHERIFF HARTWELL

Is that so?

HILDY JOHNSON

Yes.

WALTER BURNS

I will see that Roosevelt hears about it.

SHERIFF HARTWELL

All right, tell him. Come on, boys, confiscate this desk.

WALTER BURNS

Your last chance. This is a federal offense, and you fellows will be accessories.

SHERIFF HARTWELL

We'll take a chance on that. Go ahead, boys.

Two of the reporters go to help move the desk.

WALTER BURNS

All right.

POLICEMAN

Open up this door.

Mrs. Baldwin comes in accompanied by a policeman.

HILDY JOHNSON

Mother, I am glad to see you. Are you all right? I've
been . . .

MRS. BRUCE BALDWIN

That's the man that did it, right there.

SHERIFF HARTWELL

What's the idea here?

POLICEMAN

This lady claims she's been kidnapped.

SHERIFF HARTWELL

What?

MRS. BRUCE BALDWIN

They dragged me all the way down the stairs. And put
me . . .

SHERIFF HARTWELL

Just a minute. Did this man
                    (Walter)
have anything to do with it?

MRS. BALDWIN

Well, he was in charge of the whole thing. He told them to kidnap me.

WALTER BURNS

Excuse me, madam. Are you referring to me?

MRS. BALDWIN

Well, you know you did.

SHERIFF HARTWELL

What about this, Burns? Kidnapping? Huh?

WALTER BURNS

Oh, you're trying to frame me, huh? I never saw this woman before in my life.

MRS. BALDWIN

Wait, what a thing to say! I was standing right here when that girl jumped out the window.

SHERIFF HARTWELL

Call the Mayor. Get him over here right away.

WALTER BURNS

Look here, madam. Be honest. If you were out joy-riding plastered and got into some scrape, why don't you admit it, instead of accusing innocent people?

MRS. BALDWIN

You ruffian, how dare you talk like that to me?

HILDY JOHNSON

He is just a little crazy, mother.

MRS. BALDWIN

And I can tell you something more.

SHERIFF HARTWELL

Yes?

MRS. BRUCE BALDWIN

I can tell you why they did it.

SHERIFF HARTWELL

Yeah?

MRS. BRUCE BALDWIN

They had some kind of a murderer in here and they were hiding him.

SHERIFF HARTWELL

Hiding him?

MRS. BRUCE BALDWIN

Yeah.

SHERIFF HARTWELL

In here?

MRS. BRUCE BALDWIN

Yes.

WALTER BURNS

Madam, you're a cockeyed liar, and you know it!

For emphasis, Walter raps three times on the desk. Earl Williams, inside, raps back.

SHERIFF HARTWELL

What was that?

MURPHY

He's in there.

The reporters rush to their phones.

ENDICOTT

Give me the desk.

MURPHY

Give me the phone.

Sheriff Hartwell pulls out his gun.

SHERIFF HARTWELL

Stand back, everybody. Get your guns out.

HILDY JOHNSON

He's harmless.

SHERIFF HARTWELL

Don't take any chances. Shoot right through the desk.

HILDY JOHNSON

He can't hurt anybody; you've got his gun.

MRS. BALDWIN

Oh, dear! Get me out of here!

WALTER BURNS

Oh, do go on, you gray-haired old weasel.

MRS. BRUCE BALDWIN

Let me out of here.

Mrs. Baldwin rushes out the door to find her son there. He hugs her.

BRUCE BALDWIN

Mother, I have been looking all over for you. What happened?

The policeman closes the door behind them.

WILSON

Give me the desk.

SCHWARTZ

Hello, Jake. Hang on.

WALTER BURNS

Hildy, call Duffy.

SHERIFF HARTWELL

No, you don't.

WALTER BURNS

You want to see a scoop?

SCHWARTZ

In a minute.

SHERIFF HARTWELL

Now everybody.

MURPHY

Hold the wire.

SHERIFF HARTWELL

Aim right at the center.

HILDY JOHNSON

That's murder.

SHERIFF HARTWELL

All right, Carl, Frank, both of you get on each end of
the desk.

ENDICOTT

Coming up.

SHERIFF HARTWELL

We got you covered, Williams.

**Crosstalk between the Sheriff addressing Williams and the
reporters on their phones.**

MCCUE

In a minute.

SHERIFF HARTWELL

(to Williams)

Don't try to move.

MALE SPEAKER

Any time now.

SHERIFF HARTWELL

I'll count to three.

ENDICOTT

It's hot.

SHERIFF HARTWELL

One.

MURPHY

Ready for an emergency.

SHERIFF HARTWELL

Two.

MCCUE

Any second now.

SHERIFF HARTWELL

Three! Up with it.

They roll up the desk to find Williams.

SHERIFF HARTWELL

I got you, Williams.

EARL WILLIAMS

Go ahead, shoot me.

SHERIFF HARTWELL

Come on here.

MURPHY

Earl Williams just captured in the press room in the criminal courts building, hiding in a desk.

POLICEMAN

Come on, on your feet.

Williams gets out of the desk, and two policemen haul him off.

SHERIFF HARTWELL

Come on, boys. Don't try any funny stuff.

WILSON

(into the phone)

Williams was unconscious when they opened the desk.

MURPHY

(into the phone)

Williams put up a desperate struggle, but the police overpowered him.

ENDICOTT

(into the phone)

He offered no resistance.

MCCUE

(into the phone)

He tried to shoot it out with the cops, but his gun wouldn't work.

SCHWARTZ

(into the phone)

He broke through a whole cordon of police . . .

(into the phone)

Duffy, the Morning Post turned Williams over to the sheriff.

SHERIFF HARTWELL

Put the cuffs on these people.

A police officer handcuffs Hildy and Walter.

MURPHY

The Sheriff led the Williams capture' hold on.

ENDICOTT

The Sheriff was chasing a mysterious telephone call, which gave away Williams' hiding place.

MURPHY

Where's the old lady? Where'd she go?

WILSON

She went out.

ALL REPORTERS

Out! Call you back.

The reporters rush out, leaving Walter, Hildy, and the Sheriff alone with a policeman.

SHERIFF HARTWELL

(into a phone)

Hello, Gary, give me the warden's office, quick.

WALTER BURNS

WALTER BURNS

Hartwell, you're going to wish you'd never been born.

SHERIFF HARTWELL

Oh, am I?

The Mayor comes in.

SHERIFF HARTWELL

Hello, Fred.

MAYOR

Well, fine work, Pete. You certainly delivered the goods. I'm proud of you.

SHERIFF HARTWELL

Looks kind of natural, don't it?

MAYOR

A sight for sore eyes.

SHERIFF HARTWELL

Aiding an escaped criminal and a little charge of kidnapping . . . What's that? Well, that's the jail. There must be somebody there.

MAYOR

Well, it looks like about then years at least for you two birds.

WALTER BURNS

Does it?

HILDY JOHNSON

And if you think you've got the Morning Post licked, it's time for you to get out of town.

MAYOR

Whistling in the dark. Well, that isn't going to help you this time; you're through.

WALTER BURNS

Listen, the last man who said that to me was Archie Leach just a week before he cut his throat.

SHERIFF HARTWELL

Is that so?

WALTER BURNS

We've been in worse jams, haven't we, Hildy?

HILDY JOHNSON

No.

WALTER BURNS

You forget the power that always watches over the Morning Post.

MAYOR

That's not with you now.

SHERIFF HARTWELL

Hello, this is Hartwell. I've caught him. Yes, Williams. Single-handed. We proceed with the hanging per schedule.

WALTER BURNS

You are going to be in office exactly two days more.

HILDY JOHNSON

And we're going to start pulling your nose off that feedbag.

SHERIFF HARTWELL

I will tell what you will be doing.

WALTER BURNS

What?

SHERIFF HARTWELL

You'll be, uh . . .

WALTER BURNS

Come on, make up your mind.

SHERIFF HARTWELL

Making brooms in the state penitentiary.

(into the phone)

Hello, Joe. This is Hartwell. I want you to come over to my office right away. Yes. I've just captured a couple of important birds and I want you to take the confession.

WALTER BURNS

(into the phone)

Duffy, get Liebowitz!

MAYOR

All the lawyers in the world aren't going to help you now.

WALTER BURNS

Listen, you are talking to the Morning Post.

MAYOR

Oh, the power of the press.

WALTER BURNS

Listen, bigger men than you have found out what the power of the press is—presidents, kings.

Joe Pettibone lumbers into the office. For some reason, he still has his umbrella open, and it catches in the door, impeding his entrance.

JOE PETTIBONE

Here is the reprieve.

MAYOR

Oh, I say, you are insane! Get out of here.

JOE PETTIBONE

Oh, you can't bribe me. My wife won't . . .

SHERIFF HARTWELL

Get out of here, you.

JOE PETTIBONE

Oh, no, I won't. Here's the reprieve.

HILDY JOHNSON

What!

JOE PETTIBONE

I don't want to be a city sealer, my wife . . .

MAYOR

Who is this man?

SHERIFF HARTWELL

Throw him out, Frank.

HILDY JOHNSON

Wait, just a minute. Wait a minute. Who's trying to bribe you?

JOE PETTIBONE

They wouldn't take this.

MAYOR

He's insane.

WALTER BURNS

What did I tell you? An unseen power!

MAYOR

What do you mean by coming in here with a cock-and-bull story like that?

SHERIFF HARTWELL

Free him up. He's an impostor.

MAYOR

Arrest him.

HILDY JOHNSON

Just a minute! Trying to hang an innocent man just to win election!

WALTER BURNS

That's murder.

SHERIFF HARTWELL

That's a lie.

MAYOR

Never saw him before.

JOE PETTIBONE

If I was to tell my wife . . .

HILDY JOHNSON

What's your name?

JOE PETTIBONE

Pettibone. Joe Pettibone.

WALTER BURNS

When did you deliver this first, Mr. Pettibone?

HILDY JOHNSON

Who did you talk to?

JOE PETTIBONE

They started right in bribing me.

HILDY JOHNSON

Who's they?

Pettibone points toward the Sheriff and the Mayor.

JOE PETTIBONE

Those, them.

MAYOR

That's absurd, on the face of it. Walter, he's talking like a child.

WALTER BURNS

Out of the mouth of babes.

JOE PETTIBONE

A baby.

MAYOR

He is insane, drunk, or something. Why? If this unfortunate man Williams has really been reprieved, I'm personally tickled to death, aren't you, Pete?

HILDY JOHNSON

Oh, go on. You would hang your own mother to be reelected.

MAYOR

That's a horrible thing to say about anybody, Miss Johnson.

WALTER BURNS

Oh, you're marvelous. Take a look at that.

MAYOR

Walter, you're an intelligent man.

WALTER BURNS

Uh, never mind that. Now let's have your story, Mr. Pettibone.

JOE PETTIBONE

Well, nineteen years ago, I married Mrs. Pettibone.

WALTER BURNS

Skip all that.

JOE PETTIBONE

Well, she wasn't Mrs. Pettibone then . . .

WALTER BURNS

No.

JOE PETTIBONE

She was one of the Jones.

The Mayor has been examining the reprieve.

MAYOR

Sheriff! This document is authentic, and Earl Williams has been reprieved, and our commonwealth has been saved the painful necessity of shedding blood.

WALTER BURNS

Easier said than done. Get off the soapbox. Save that for the Tribune.

MAYOR

Pete, take those handcuffs off my friends.

The Sheriff obeys.

SHERIFF HARTWELL

I am just going . . .

MAYOR

I am amazed that you're doing a thing like that.

WALTER BURNS

Isn't it awful?

MAYOR

Walter, you don't know how badly I feel.

WALTER BURNS

No.

MAYOR

No excuse at all for Pete to fly off the handle.

SHERIFF HARTWELL

I was only doing my duty. Nothing personal, you know.

HILDY JOHNSON

That's all right.

MAYOR

What'd you say your name was?

JOE PETTIBONE

Pettibone was . . . Yes, here's a picture of my wife.

He moves to take his wife's picture out of his pocket. Before he can:

MAYOR

Yeah, fine-looking woman.

JOE PETTIBONE

But you haven't seen her yet.

MAYOR

Yeah. Well, she's all right.

JOE PETTIBONE

Oh, well, she's good enough for me. If I was to tell my wife . . .

MAYOR

I understand perfectly, Mr. Pettibone, and as long as I'm mayor, why . . .

WALTER BURNS

It ought to be about three more hours, I'd say.

HILDY JOHNSON

That's long enough for us to get out a special edition asking for your recall.

WALTER BURNS

And your arrest. You know, you little boys ought to get about ten years of peace, I think.

HILDY JOHNSON

Yep.

MAYOR

Don't make any hasty decisions, Mr. Burns. You might run into a thumping big libel suit.

HILDY JOHNSON

You might run into the governor.

MAYOR

Why? My old friend the governor and I understand each other perfectly.

SHERIFF HARTWELL

Yes, and so do I.

MAYOR

(to Hartwell)

So you do what? And now, Mr. Pettibone, if you'll come along with us, we'll take you over to the warden's office and deliver this reprieve. Come along, Pete.

JOE PETTIBONE

If I was to tell my wife . . .

MAYOR

You won't have to.

The Mayor, Sheriff, and Pettibone go out.

WALTER BURNS

Wait until those two future jailbirds read the Morning Post tomorrow.

HILDY JOHNSON

It was a tight squeeze, though. That's the worst jam we've been in a long time.

Walter picks up the phone.

WALTER BURNS

(into the phone)

Yeah. What? Well, where is he? Get him.

HILDY JOHNSON

Remember the time we stole old lady Haggerty's stomach off the coroner's physician?

WALTER BURNS

(to Hildy)

Anytime you need this guy, he's never there.

HILDY JOHNSON

We proved she'd been poisoned in the water.

WALTER BURNS

Mm-hmm. Yeah.

HILDY JOHNSON

We had to hide out for a week. Do you remember that? In the Shoreland Hotel? That's where, I mean, how we . . .

WALTER BURNS

We could have gone to jail for that too. You know that? Oh, yes, maybe you're right, Hildy, it's a bad business. Well, you're going to be better off, so you'd better get going.

HILDY JOHNSON

Where am I going to go?

WALTER BURNS

Well, to Bruce, of course.

HILDY JOHNSON

You know he's gone. He took the nine o'clock . . .

WALTER BURNS

I just sent him a wire. He'll be waiting at the station when you get into Albany. Go on.

(into the phone)

What? Like, why doesn't that guy ever fully put in there?

HILDY JOHNSON

Maybe . . .

WALTER BURNS

Keep going, Hildy.

HILDY JOHNSON

Keep going, gigger. What is that with you?

WALTER BURNS

Wait a minute. Look, honey, can't you understand? I'm trying to do something noble for once in my life. Now get out of here before I change my mind. Come on.

HILDY JOHNSON

But Walter, listen . . .

WALTER BURNS

It's tough enough now.

HILDY JOHNSON

Just a minute.

WALTER BURNS

I have sent the fellow a wire; he'll be waiting when you get there. Come on.

HILDY JOHNSON

Who'll write the story?

WALTER BURNS

I'll do it myself. I'll be happy to, because you didn't . . .

HILDY JOHNSON

It's my story. I'd kind of like to think that it . . .

WALTER BURNS

(into the phone)

Hello. Oh, at last, Duffy.

HILDY JOHNSON

I get it, Walter, the same old act, isn't it? Trying to push me out of here, thinking I'll be stupid enough to want to stay.

WALTER BURNS

Oh, I know I deserve that, Hildy.

(into the phone)

Wait a minute, Duffy.

(to Hildy)

But this is one time you're wrong. Look, honey, when you walk out that door, part of me will go right with you. But a whole new world's going to open up for you. I made fun of Bruce and Albany and all that kind of thing. You know why?

HILDY JOHNSON

Why?

WALTER BURNS

I was jealous. I was sore because he can offer you the kind of life I can't give you. That's what you want, honey.

HILDY JOHNSON

I could stay and do the story and take the train in the morning. Just make . . .

WALTER BURNS

Oh, forget it. Come on. Come on. Goodbye, dear, and good luck.

(into the phone)

Well, Duffy. Hello, this is how it goes so far. Oh, just a minute.

Another phone rings; Walter answers it. Hildy is on her way out with her overcoat and suitcase.

WALTER BURNS

(into the phone)

Hello. Who? Hildy Johnson? No, she just left.

HILDY JOHNSON

I'm still here. I can take it.

WALTER BURNS

Hang on a minute.

HILDY JOHNSON

(into the phone)

Hildy Johnson speaking. The fourth precinct police station? Well, put him on. Bruce, I thought you were on your way to Albany. What for?

Bruce is talking from a phone in the police station.

BRUCE BALDWIN

For having counterfeit money.

HILDY JOHNSON

Counterfeit money?

WALTER BURNS

Hold on a minute, Duffy.

HILDY JOHNSON

Oh, where did you get it? I gave it to you? Oh, right.

Hildy starts to cry. Walter is about to go out but stops.

WALTER BURNS

Oh, honey. Honey, don't, don't cry, please. Oh, come on. I didn't mean to make you cry, honey. What's the matter with you? You never cried before. Hildy.

HILDY JOHNSON

I thought you were really sending me away with Bruce. I didn't know you had him locked up. I thought you were on the level for once, that you were just standing by and letting me go off with him and not doing a thing about it.

WALTER BURNS

Oh, come on, honey. What did you think I was—a chump?

HILDY JOHNSON

I mean, I thought you didn't like me.

WALTER BURNS

What were you thinking with?

HILDY JOHNSON

I don't know. But what are you standing there gawking for? We have to get him out of jail. Send Louie down with some honest money, and send him back to Albany, where he belongs.

WALTER BURNS

Sure.

(into the phone)

Hello, Duffy, everything's changed. Tell Louie to stand by; we're coming over the office. Nah, don't worry about the story. Hildy is going to write it. Plus she's not quitting. She never intended to. We're going to get married.

HILDY JOHNSON

Oh, can we go on a honeymoon this time, Walter?

WALTER BURNS

Sure. Hey, Duffy, you're going to be managing editor. No. No. Not permanently. Just for the two weeks we're away on the honeymoon.

HILDY JOHNSON

Oh, what?

WALTER BURNS

(into the phone)

I don't know where we're going? Where are we going?

HILDY JOHNSON

Niagara Falls.

WALTER BURNS

(into the phone)

Niagara Falls, Duffy.

HILDY JOHNSON

Two weeks, Walter.

WALTER BURNS

(into the phone)

Sure, you've earned it. What? What? Strike? What strike? Where? Albany. Well, I know it's on the way, Duffy, but I can't ask Hildy to . . .

HILDY JOHNSON

All right. We'll go honeymoon in Albany.

She is clutching her suitcase to her chest.

WALTER BURNS

(into the phone)

Okay, Duffy.

Walter hangs up. He and Hildy walk out of the press room. She is still clutching her suitcase to her chest.

WALTER BURNS

Well, isn't that a coincidence? We're going to Albany. I wonder if Bruce can put us up, and say . . . why don't you carry that in your hand?

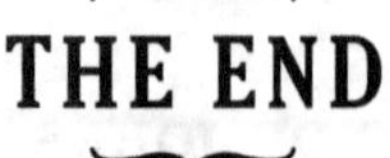

THE END

www.ingramcontent.com/pod-product-compliance
Lightning Source LLC
Chambersburg PA
CBHW060401310726

48976CB00003B/899